the Atelier

Glenn Haybittle

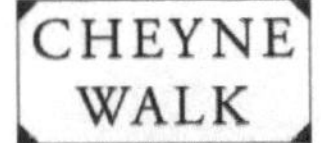

Published by Cheyne Walk 2019

Published by Cheyne Walk

www.cheynewalk.co

ISBN- 13: 978-1-9999682-2-9

The least of things with a meaning is worth more in life than the greatest of things without it.

— Carl Jung

I

Regno

1

Jared Regis looked up at the woman of carved stone, studying her as if she were a chess piece. One of the two threshold guardians on the north side of the Ponte Santa Trìnita, she clasped a bundle of ripe grain to her breast and held herself apart. Jared though could not quite clear his mind of his wife's reproaches. He looked from the statue of bountiful harvest to the threadbare grass of the riverbank succumbing to winter's mud and slime. The river, thick and clouded with churned-up residue, raged with some unresolved conflict. The momentum of the moon-governed tide had dislodged what was moored, submerged and hidden. Jared reached the statue of the shivering naked male on the far side and made his way towards the weir over which the full force of the Arno tumbled.

The upstairs backroom at the studio was Jared's inner sanctum. In an arched niche high in the wall a cast of Venus presided over his Descent from the Cross. The last time he had worked on it was a few days ago when, down on his knees, he had painted an emerald stone around the neck of the Virgin Mary. His wife had posed for the Madonna and lay in a faint at the bottom of the canvas. The swirling dark background threatened to engulf her. This was the third time he had unconsciously painted his wife unconscious. The third time he had shown her in a state of slumber, unable or unwilling to open her eyes. This was one of the mysteries of his painting. His eye moved to the figure of Christ on the cross who bore a subtle resemblance to Jared himself. The sky had split open above Christ's head. His left hand was still nailed to the cross, his right arm stretched down towards the unconscious Madonna. The living Christ was embraced by the beautiful Magdalene who gripped his leg beneath the knee around which she had entwined her long dark curls. Jared's daughter, the ten-year-old Cordelia, had posed as a child who held the Madonna's hand but, turned away from her mother, was gazing up at Magdalene, the fallen woman. Only now did Jared notice a note of mistrust in the highlight of his child's eye.

Jared opened the copy of the Bible given to him by his father. *If thou seekest her as silver, and searchest for her as for hid treasure; Then shalt thou understand the fear of the Lord, and find the knowledge of God.* Jared enjoyed opening the Bible at random and reading the first few lines on which his eyes alighted. *If thou seekest her as silver...* What did that mean exactly? *Her* instantly evoked an erotic undertow. *She* was the vision which set him down before the ocean of all his sustaining longings. *She* could never be for him merely an abstract principle. *She* was forever and always personified in physical form as the muse. Was the problem then that his wife had ceased to be his muse? He had given some thought to the idea of adding two panels to his Descent from the Cross - on these he would depict Adam and Eve. No muse though had appeared, no female model posing nude for his students was quite appropriate to the idea he had in mind.

As Jared stepped up closer to his picture, a voice, English, well-educated, slightly affected in tone and unfamiliar, resounded through the corridor of the deconsecrated church.

"If I'm not mistaken, that's Raphael leading Tobias and his dog on the plaque outside, off to cure his old father's blindness with the fish," said the dark-haired man who pushed aside the drapes of Jared's studio. "Forgive me for intruding. My name, by the way, is Sparks. Damien Sparks."

Jared shook the man's hand. He was wearing a russet sweater beneath a black sheepskin coat.

"This building," said Jared, "used to be a church dedicated to the Archangel Raphael, healer and guide of wayfarers."

"Now it's an atelier, I believe. This building, you see, played a part in my youth. I attended one or two parties here in the sixties. That was before I went into law, when I was still idealistic." The man, lit a cigarette with a match and blew out a dissolving circle of smoke. "I remember there was a huge Buddha statue up there which I see has been replaced by the goddess of love. The parties here were rather wild. Usually they didn't end until Venus, in her guise as the morning star, was fading from the sky. A woman was raped at one of them, downstairs somewhere I believe. That caused quite a rumpus among the English community at the time. In those days, as I recall, this building was believed to be haunted. An angry woman was the general hypothesis. I don't suppose you've ever experienced her - the angry woman?"

"I thought all women were angry nowadays," said Jared with a smile.

"I'll never understand women. One of the reasons I'm retracing my steps is a hiatus in my relations with my wife. She possesses an absolutely brilliant mind and thus it's very difficult ever to win arguments. She's given me permission to have an affair. Says I ought to sow some wild oats. Her only clause is that it must be an affair with a girl no older than twenty-two. Her reasoning is that I'll soon grow bored without intellectual stimulus and that girls are still mentally unformed until they reach twenty-three. I suppose that's rather an arbitrary statement but those were her words. She believes I will be saved by a sacrifice on her part."

"So you've come to Florence to have a fling?"

"No. The older I get the less interested I become in libidinal frisson. Among other things, I've come with the idea of purchasing property in Chiantishire."

"Not this particular piece of property, I take it?"

"No, no. I'm no artist and I'm certainly not interested in moral responsibilities. Any claim I had to moral high ground went to the dogs when I defended the Prince of Darkness. That's what I call the most infamous of my clients. He pays me a yearly annuity for a scrape I got him out of. Therefore, I'm still, you might say, in his pay."

"The Prince of Darkness?"

"My private joke," said Damien Sparks. He now turned to look at Jared's painting for the first time. "So you're a great fan of chiaroscuro. Isn't that merely old hat?"

"I paint from nature; I paint what I see," said Jared.

"I'm not sure I trust these formulas for capturing beauty. We've had golden sections, squares, circles, S shapes. Each one becomes slavish in its own way. Artistic doctrine has a well-recorded history of inhibiting creativity. Actually, I recently acquired a rather nice piece of work. It was a painting on a piece of old plywood. Rather Chinese in its effect of leading the observer towards an idea of the purification of spirit. I've also just purchased two paintings by a London artist called Babb. They're both yellow – primrose yellow squares. I find them fascinating."

"Shelley said poets are the hierophants of an unapprehended inspiration. What kind of inspiration is a yellow square?"

"Inspiration is for artists. I'm a lawyer. So," the man said, after looking deeply into Jared's shy blue eyes, "a charge of magus might be levelled at you? What is it you teach your students? To paint what they see?"

"Any depicted idea of beauty depends on seeing the whole, and then choosing what to leave out as well as what to put in. Painting has as much to do with evolving consciousness as training the eye."

"Quantum theory has it that we change things by observing them. So aren't you really just seeing what you want to see? Which is to say, reality as the old masters perceived it." The barrister turned his attention back to Jared's painting. "But tell me, why is the Virgin wearing an emerald stone?"

Jared himself was not sure why he had painted the stone

around his wife's neck. It was his gift to her on her fortieth birthday. The green stone summoned to his mind an image of the grail stone and his idea was that it would act as a kind of talisman. He found it in a town where he had gone to visit a Romanesque church. There was a scallop shell on the door, a testament to the pilgrims who had used these shells in which to collect alms.

The interior of the church, at first glance, had no floor and resembled the kind of spectacle the mind produces in sleep. The arches and the roof all lay at his feet as well as over his head. The floor was entirely covered in mirrors. His initial reaction was mistrust as though he were about to be ensnared in some fatuous modern performance art from which even his beloved Romanesque churches were no longer immune. He thought about turning his back on the experience, especially when he saw a sign saying that shoes had to be removed. He picked up a leaflet. The leaflet was entitled, *Quod superius, sicut quod inferius* - As above, so below. There was a primitive drawing of two snakes forming a double spiral around a rod. They were on the verge of attacking one another. He read only a fragment of the text alluding to the *Tabula smaragdina*, the emerald tablet, on which the essence of the alchemical opus was inscribed in thirteen sentences from Hermes Trismegistus. He walked slowly across the glass towards the transept with the church's double row of arches soaring both above and below him. The world had been turned upside down. He felt as though he was walking on water. All the weight in his body dissolved and he succumbed to a sensation of being suspended ethereally between two surfaces, two worlds. His progress across the glass and its disorientating duplications was accompanied every so often by images of an embryo developing inside a womb. Something was trying to rebirth him. Something was trying to make him experience a reality which denied hard analysis.

He saw the stone in the window of a shop while walking back to his car. It had the form of an Egyptian scarab and its markings etched out a primitive cross. Diane wore the necklace for a month, seeming to take great pleasure from it, and then put it away in a drawer. He later discovered that the emerald stone was the jewel that fell to earth from Lucifer's crown when he was cast out of heaven.

"Do you know why you do everything you do?" asked Jared in response to Damien Sparks' question. "The stone appeared and I painted it."

The barrister was now looking closely at Jared's portrait of a blind man. He then turned back to Jared with the same studious look on his face. "I don't suppose," he said, picking up a jar of honey-coloured medium and holding it up to the light, "for old times' sake, you'd care to show me round the downstairs part of the studio?"

There being no direct access between the upstairs and downstairs floors, they descended the narrow marble stairs to the street below. Yesterday it had snowed. A rare occurrence in Florence. Only pools of slush remained now. Jared noticed a single fresh yellow rose placed on the tabernacle to the Madonna across the street before he led Damien Sparks through the large wooden door. Beneath a high vaulted ceiling the room was cluttered with easels and model stands. Small plaster casts lined the shelves - an orderless miscellanea of angels, ballerinas, holy virgins and nymphs collecting dust.

"I seem to recall there being talk of a crypt somewhere down here. You haven't located it, I suppose."

"There's a kind of trap door beneath that rug over there which leads down into a small cellar."

"No, this was a proper crypt. People were said to have hidden there during the war."

"Perhaps you should speak to the owner of the building, Guido Locatelli. His family has owned this building for generations. They were all sculptors. He might know where the crypt is."

Jared flicked on the switch but no light was forthcoming.

The walls of the old church climbed a vast distance until they disappeared into the penumbra beneath the wooden rafters high above. Hoists which once upon a time must have shifted huge slabs of marble were adorned with rams' heads. Diffused luminosity filtered down through the large glass window and lent to the many white casts scattered everywhere a disconcerting intimacy. The two men stood in the shadow of an angel with poised wings.

"It's like the building's memory in here," said the barrister. "I was here in 1966, the year of the flood. Did you know there was another serious flood in 1333? Do you go in for number games? I personally have a soft spot for that kind of thing. 33 and 66 might lead one to deduct that the next flood will be in 99."

The light now flickered on, bringing into focus the far wall where chipped grey columns supported a series of three arches beneath one of which hung a crucified Christ. They were standing in a vast neglected warehouse of casts.

"I believe our underworld vault is over there, somewhere behind those statues. I have a feeling that's where this woman was raped."

"Why are you so interested in this rape?"

The barrister, having led Jared over to a colossal reclining stone river god, said, "I suppose because in a way it decided my fate. It marked the end of an era."

"You knew the woman involved?"

"She was an extremely attractive though rather unconscious woman, if you know what I mean. And, as I recall, it was believed in certain quarters that a child was born."

2

Drifts and flurries of snow circled the air as if awakening one another. With the ferment of his dreams subsiding Rowan Fisher looked out on a white world with here and there an orange blaze of colour, like smudges of pollen. Before long, the night train from Paris would be pulling into Santa Maria Novella. From midnight until six in the morning he had been out in the corridor watching worlds come into visibility that had no knowledge or need of him. He saw the reflection of his own face, spectral, bloodless, imposed on barren sunflower fields and vineyards preparing next year's harvest beneath the frosted soil.

It was early morning when Rowan walked from the station to Piazza Santa Maria Novella. He sat down on the icy steps of the loggia facing the Dominican church. He could not gaze for long at the marble façade without being driven back into his own mind. The virgin seal of snow crowning the city's rooftops drew attention to the history of the stones, the struggles of blood and line they had witnessed. Rowan heard a bell, which like light after rain, gave to the moment an undertow. He picked up his bags that contained everything of value he possessed in the world and went in search of a hotel for the night.

By evening the snow had melted. The streets were darker than those of London. Giotto's tower and Brunelleschi's dome stood out stark and galvanised against the backdrop of hills. Clouds patterned like fish scales made of the sky a tidal labyrinth of submerged lights. The waxing moon above San Miniato appeared to dissolve in its own mercurial glow. After crossing the river he entered a bar in Piazza Santa Croce and ordered a glass of red wine. At the next table two American men were in loud debate.

"You're a great draughtsman, Frank, always have been, but now you're selling your soul doing frescoes for American banks."

"Why do always have to pass judgement, Jared? Hey," said the more rugged of the two men catching Rowan's eye and addressing him. "Has anyone ever told you that you look like Dante? The statue of him outside Santa Croce, I mean."

Rowan smiled, not sure if this was a compliment or not.

"Did you know the statue of Dante used to be in the centre of the piazza? They moved it after the flood. But what are you doing in this beautiful city?"

"I just arrived today. I'm about to work at the British Institute."

"In that case," said Jared, "you'll meet Tim Garnett. He's the head librarian."

"I'm going to live in his house in the country."

"Tim and Rachel's house? I've been there. Do you know Tim and Rachel then?"

"I've never met them."

"Tim's a very nice man. If you need any extra money I could find you some work modelling at my studio," said Jared. "My students are always looking for portrait models."

"You've got a great face to draw. I'd sure like to draw you but I'm heading back to France tomorrow," said Frank.

Rowan, after promising Jared he would stop by at the studio, returned to his *pensione*. Alone in his room, he went to the window and, looking out over the orange rooftops of the city, he began thinking of his motive for coming to Florence. His true parents existed in his mind as intuitions or phantoms rather than memories and as such he could no more identify himself with them than he could with any other person he did not know. He had no idea what, if any, hopes he was fulfilling or disappointing; he had no ancestral castle returning him to his origins. The only information he had managed to obtain about his mother was in a letter he carried with him in his bag. It had been addressed to his adoptive parents via a London solicitor.

November 8, 1966
Via Porta Rossa, 20
Firenze

Dear Mr. and Mrs. Fisher,

I am writing this letter to inform you of the death of Rowan's mother. She died in the dreadful flood that devastated Florence this week. I know you never met Ivana and know nothing about the unhappy circumstances which forced her to give up her son. What these circumstances were she pledged me to not reveal.

In her will Ivana left a request that a ring which belonged to her father be bequeathed to Rowan on her death. This ring I shall send to Ivana's solicitors in the hope that they will forward it to you.

Yours sincerely,
Bianca Monaco

Rowan remembered the day his mother had told him she was actually his adoptive mother. Displays of feeling had never come easy to either of them, and his mother's only concession to imparting information out of the ordinary was in the historical setting she chose as its backdrop; they were walking in the gardens of Hampton Court. The news came as no great catalytic shock. He was still shy, still inclined to replace action with thought, a stranger to self-assertion and confident poise. He felt what he needed to do was to get up at dawn and tramp through early morning mist and dew - from field to field with the innocence of sheep and cows as company, experience physically the birth of a new day.

3

The blue bus spluttered off leaving Rowan alone in a travel brochure landscape of cultivated hills and silvered olive groves. He climbed a slope on the crest of which rose an old Benedictine abbey. Earlier he had visited the house in via Porta Rossa from where Bianca Monaco's letter had been sent. The door had been green and there were a dozen or so bells. He had studied the faded brass names in search of a Bianca Monaco but in vain.

Tim and Rachel Garnett lived in a renovated stone farmhouse with a small tower and many deft artisan annotations. That books were piled haphazardly everywhere and there proliferated what, in the world of his adoptive parents, would constitute disorder reassured Rowan that there would be a minimum of stifling formalities to go through. Rachel quickly made him feel at ease. Vigorously elegant, she had a replenishing air about her. It was like she had imbibed the wisdom of both the soil and the stars and she created an atmosphere in which it was difficult to feel clumsy. Rowan instinctively warmed to her.

Tim, her husband, arrived later. He was an academic elusive man with no apparent axes to grind and no obvious prejudices demanding indulgence. Often he looked bemused at what went on around him, as if caught in the act of relinquishing responsibility to a tide which continually ebbed away from where he stood.

Halfway through lunch Tim said, "There's been more talk today of getting some feisty career woman in to make the library more economically viable. Apparently, we're out of touch with the modern world. We have to *maximise our assets.*"

"You *are* out of touch with the modern world, Dad, and that's the large part of the library's charm," said Benedict, the eldest son. "The lights often don't work downstairs and how many books are there that were written after the second world war? About three - and they're usually books about books written before the second world war. You have twenty-seven different editions of *Great Expectations*; I counted once."

"We're only allowed to buy a limited number of new books a month."

"So you get in another edition of *Great Expectations*?"

"They're donated to the library. Everyone who dies in Florence has a copy of *Great Expectations*."

"Do you have great expectations, Rowan?" asked Beatrice, who was seventeen.

Rowan felt the whole table's attention focused on him.

"One always wants to know what will happen next. Having something to look forward to is the only kind of happiness I can imagine," he said.

Beatrice sat up erect in her chair like a flower seeking sunlight. "So you believe like Proust that happiness only exists in the imagination or the memory?"

"Stop being so pedantic, Beatrice," said her mother. "You sound like the Spanish Inquisition. Rowan's trying to eat his meal. Do young girls always have to show off? I wonder if I was like you at your age."

"Can't you remember?" asked the younger daughter Cecilia shyly.

"When you get to my age the mind becomes a marketplace of fact and fiction. Do you know anyone in Florence?" asked Rachel.

"No, not really. Although I have met an American artist who runs an atelier here."

"Jared Regis," said Tim.

"Is he still working on that Descent of his?" asked Benedict. "The other day I bumped into him and he asked me if I knew what the harrowing of hell was."

"One thing that always strikes me about Jared," said Rachel, ladling out more food into her husband's bowl, "is that though he's an incredibly knowledgeable man he's too quick to take exception and comes across at times as being emotionally immature."

"Aren't all clever men like that? They develop their minds at the expense of their emotions. Isn't that why erudite scholars often end up falling in love with nineteen-year-old blonde bimbos?" said Beatrice.

"Do they?" asked Tim, smiling.

"Of course they do. It's a well-known fact, Dad."

"Jared has more energy than most men half his age," said Tim.

"Nervous energy," said Rachel, "which would be rather exhausting to any woman who lived with him, though I dare say it's a wonderful attribute where the students are concerned."

"I would imagine any man called upon to personify a creed will end up becoming a victim of that creed," said Rowan. "To stand up for an existing idea means denying yourself personal evolution to some extent. It's the idea of the stern father or the defender of the realm. Look what happened to King Lear when he became soft."

"He lost his mind," said Beatrice.

"And his ability to see."

"The poor man did though have rather unpleasant daughters," smiled Tim.

"Not like you, eh Dad?" said Cecilia, once again defying her shy self-consciousness.

After lunch Rowan and Rachel went for a walk together, accompanied by the family's four dogs. They strolled down the pitted road and then cut across a vineyard towards the lake. The line upon line of black vines looked like the charred remains of arrested dancers.

During their long walk they passed a plaque on the ruins of an old wall commemorating eleven partisans executed there during the war.

"It's difficult to imagine this landscape swarming with dangers and fear," said Rowan. "Everything looks so peaceful now."

"It's a lovely place to live. It was almost an act of divine providence, us finding our house. Tim and I lived in a cramped little flat in Florence and didn't have much money. I was pregnant with Beatrice and clearly we had to find somewhere more spacious. We were going to see another house quite a way from here but took the wrong exit on the autostrada and literally bumped into this house. And it was unbelievably cheap. You'll find things like that happen quite a lot in Florence." She pulled down an olive branch and let it run through her fingers. "Do you believe in fate?"

"Absolutely. I've always felt attracted to Florence, ever since I was a child. And what is fate if not attraction?"

"I think that's true. Florence is a very fateful city. Often one has a sense of Florence answering one back, if you know what I mean."

Instead of returning to the house with Rachel, Rowan walked down to the lake, his shoes sinking into the mud and sodden bracken. He sat down near the water's edge. Having smoked a cigarette he was about to leave when he became aware of rustling foliage behind him. A girl appeared and walked to the edge of the water. She hadn't noticed him. He watched her remove her black cardigan. Her faintly tanned back was now naked save for a black strap visible in part beneath her long dark hair. She reached behind for its clasp. He was now caught in two minds. Should he remain quiet or should he save later embarrassment by making his presence known now? It was Rowan's nature to disclaim advantages.

"*Ma non fai un bagno con questo freddo*?" he called out. The girl swivelled around on her hips.

"You can speak English, if you like," she said.

"You're not going for a swim in this weather, are you?" he repeated with smiling eyes.

"I haven't seen you before," she said.

"If it comes to that, I haven't seen you before either."

"Do you want to swim? I came here to swim."

"I can't swim."

"I can teach you. It's very easy. It is just a question of trust and overcoming fear."

"I'm not very good at overcoming fear."

"I can see that by the way you sit in your body. Do you want a fig? I've got some in my bag."She made a motion towards her bag leaning forward and showing the curves of her small breasts.

"What's your name?"

"Kira."

"Do you live around here?"

"Over there." She pointed vaguely towards the deep winter shadows beyond the thickets on the far slope of the valley.

"And what do you do?"

"I study dance. At a school in via Ghibellina." She folded her arms over her chest and shivered. "I think I won't swim now."

"Is that my fault?"

She put back on her cardigan and stood staring at him while he sat peeling off a slither of willow bark.

"How can I get hold of you?" he asked when she showed signs of leaving him.

"You can't," she said. "You'll have to wait until I come swimming again, though maybe next time you will have to come swimming too."

4

Eve arrived the day of carnival, the night of the black moon. She was biting into a green apple as she ascended the marble stairs of the deconsecrated church in Borgo San Frediano.

"So you'd be willing to pose?" Jared asked the girl from Alaska who, as though brandishing a staff of bells, created around herself a wake of heightened attention.

"If I could draw half days too that would be perfect."

Jared showed Mercy around the studio. He was eager for her approval. Women were dangerous to him until he was sure he had their admiration. Mercy repaid this demand with interest. The school, she said, was her dream come true. She enjoyed resorting to breathless exclamations of enthusiasm. He unveiled his Descent from the Cross. He told her to stand back in order to see the overall composition better and explained his theory of the limited palette. Mercy told him that his was the most sensual Christ she had ever seen in her life.

"He is rather sensual, isn't he?" said Jared, pleased but mastering his pleasure. "I concentrated on the torso. That's what matters - the body of Christ. It's also a reference to Adam - the ribs, I mean. Christ is about to descend into the underworld to redeem Adam and Eve. This picture is made to go above an altar, though it's rather too daring to be accepted by any church. Christ's body is the Host."

"He's beautiful. If only he existed in real life, I'd marry him," Mercy said, touching Jared on the shoulder. The contact surprised him into physical self-consciousness. "I think you've painted my ideal man, Jared."

"Are you turning my Christ into a pin-up, Mercy?" Jared laughed. Mercy however let it be known with an expression of solemnity that she was living a sacred moment. She lowered her eyes as if entering into a state of holy communion.

"Jared, can I ask you something personal?"

"I don't see why not," said Jared, bending down to wipe off a brush hair he had noticed on Magdalene's foot.

"Do you believe in God?"

"Or the possibility of burning in hell?" he laughed, looking from Magdalene to Mercy. "Are you putting me on the spot?"

"No. Or I don't mean to."

"I've always wanted to believe in God," he said. "Sometime, when painting, I listen to Handel's *Messiah* for inspiration. There's that line, *Yet in my flesh shall I see God*. But why do you ask?"

"It's just that something happened to me when I was twelve. I had to make a vow."

"And what kind of vow was that, Mercy?"

"Oh, a vow of chastity. I swore I would remain a virgin until my wedding day. You can't imagine the frustration I have to put up with. And it's for a lifetime. You see, I already know I could never ever settle for just one man. There are so many masculine qualities that I admire and no one man could ever possess them all."

There was no irony. She was deadly serious. And it was all said with the natural exuberance of her age.

"And why did you make this vow?"

"Oh, I'd rather not talk about it." She lowered her eyes, and her hand went to the back of her neck. "Maybe when I know you better. I had a kind of vision afterwards though. It was really neat. I knew then lots of things about myself and my future. I knew I was being guided."

"So you believe in predestination?"

"I believe in God's will and God's mercy. I believe God has sent me here."

"Are you yourself God's mercy?" laughed Jared.

Mercy smiled. "Are you sure you don't want me to take my clothes off? I don't mind."

Jared was not quite sure she had said what he thought she had said. A fleeting vision of Mercy naked had passed through his mind just before she had spoken and he was now embarrassed and almost inclined to believe her endowed with psychic powers of divination.

"If I'm going to pose nude for your students, surely you need to make sure my body is suitable?"

"We'll set up the pose after class today," he said without looking at her and walked up to his picture and began studying the figure of the Virgin Mary. "I might ask you to pose for the Madonna as well. That's my wife Diane but she refuses to pose for me any more."

"That's kinda mean of her," said Mercy. "I'd be honoured to pose for you."

"It'll only be for the hands but perhaps I'll start a new painting of you. Maybe I'll paint you as Eve too. What's your feeling about posing as Eve?"

"Every woman has an Eve inside her," she said, her hands gathering up her long hair at the nape of her neck.

Jared had just finished setting up the pose Mercy was to hold for the advanced group of students. He had never before seen a model divest herself of her clothes with such intimate seductive theatre. In the high-windowed oval room she had slowly, coyly unfastened her bra as if for the sole benefit of a watching lover. Jared had watched fascinated while she lingeringly peeled off her black knickers and stood naked before them like the most willing of sacrificial victims. She had succeeded in making the men more embarrassed than she appeared to be. Even Julian Swallow, for all his rumoured exalted disdain for carnal pleasures, was clearly bewitched. Finally, a pose had been settled on. She was to be Eve holding, but not quite offering, the apple.

"I think there's a wonderful ambivalence in this pose," said

Jared, joined now by Julian and his aristocratic German girl-friend Costanza. "We're letting Eve off the hook. We're leaving it up to the viewer to decide if she's offering or withholding the apple. She's tempting but almost in spite of herself. It's her God-given beauty that is the temptation. God therefore has created a hugely volatile paradox. Is that really fair of Him? If He didn't want Adam to fall why did He make Eve so beautiful?"

"In the East there's always an element of mischievousness in the challenges the gods set us," said the ageless and good-looking Julian who before arriving in Florence had spent eighteen years in a religious community in Wales.

"God as trickster? Well, perhaps God is a trickster. Perhaps He's having fun with us. Perhaps we're His entertainment. But that's not the moral thundering God of the Old Testament."

The large oval room had been darkened and decorated for the Mardi Gras party. Jared's painting of his wife hung on the south wall above the disused fireplace. She was kneeling naked and appeared on the verge of uttering some secret combination of words. Dozens of fretted red votive candles lined the walls creating a kind of illuminated ceremonial darkness. Most people had come in costume - saints and sinners and figures from famous paintings - and were huddled in groups drinking red wine from plastic cups. Jared arrived dressed as Don Juan with white face paint and wearing a black frock coat. There was no sign of his wife. He was in good spirits and, eagerly sought as a partner by the females, danced energetically to his favourite soundtrack of Rolling Stones classics.

Damien Sparks, wearing a black sheepskin coat, arrived as midnight approached. He was talking to Mercy, who had turned up dressed as herself. Jared soon joined them.

"For the alchemists," said the barrister, "the divine centre in man was something which required careful handling if it were to be changed into a panacea. Let me show you something. Let's take a drop of this red wine and add it to this glass of water. Do you see the fog and darkness on top of the water? This is a stage in the alchemical process."

"I don't see any fog. I just see a few smoke rings."

"That's because of your optical obsession with dividing things up into the contrast between their lights and darks, Jared. You maintain you're teaching your students to see but you yourself turn a blind eye to what you don't want to see. One could argue it's all obsolete what you're doing here. Nothing but reproduction. The recycling of dead ideas."

"You don't understand what we're trying to do here," retaliated Jared with a scowl. "You make a living out of defending fraud cases in court. How moral is that, my friend? Are you not perhaps a fraud yourself, Damien? Is that why you defend frauds?"

"Who said I defend frauds? I bring things to light, Jared. That, as I see it, is my vocation. You with your chiaroscuro on the other hand smother them in shadow."

The English barrister, still holding the glass in which the water had been blemished by the wine, turned back to Mercy.

"The darkness and fog, you see, represent the first day of creation. Now we add two drops of red wine, and you will see the light coming forth from the darkness. But of course this is just ordinary wine. It needs to be done with consecrated wine."

Mercy was both fascinated and appalled, as if participating in something blasphemous.

"Seeing as though you're about to become Eve what's your idea of her?" asked Damien. "Please tell me, Mercy, what possible relevance can Eve have to modern life? When you think about it, God must have been a bit simple-minded. I mean, he creates a being who can't even resist the temptation of an apple, which quite frankly is not the most mouth-watering fruit in the world."

"The apple was a metaphor," said Mercy. "You're not supposed to take it literally. I think Eve's relevant to modern life. She was a temptress. Sometimes that's a role I catch myself playing."

"With what purpose in mind? Merely for the sheer hell of it? Excuse my language."

"I think Eve wanted to gain man's knowledge – that's why she tempted him."

The party ended at around two. Most of the students went on to a late-night drinking club; Jared found himself walking home alone.

A bell tolled, an observance thickened the night air. Jared remembered that carnival was over and it was now the first day of Lent. The beginning of Christ's forty days in the wilderness. He realised he had hardly spoken to his wife for three days and had created or participated in no rite of renewal for a long time. He felt that he had withdrawn from his own life. The bell exposed a core of vulnerability in him. He had married an unhappy woman. He wondered why. Certainly he was not con-scious of finding anything attractive about female unhappiness. Unhappy women, he supposed, spent more time thinking, more time in their minds and thus perhaps became more recognisable to male prerogatives. An unhappy woman was looking for guid-ance - a task which appealed to his sense of what a man's role in life should be.

Jared made his way to the Duomo and began circling the octagonal Baptistery. He recalled another time, several years before he had met his wife when he had stood studying the Gates of Paradise. That day there had been few people about and he was able to admire the bronze bas-reliefs at his leisure. As his eye wandered up to the expulsion of Adam and Eve he was aware of a displacement in the air over his head and then a sudden sharp pain on the back of his hand where two veins met. He looked down at his fingers and saw a snake of warm blood. By his feet there was a debris of powdered stone in which he made out the form of a broken arm. Christ's right arm had fallen, the arm of judgement.

He read in the newspaper that the arm had fallen off as a

result of cancer of the stone but why, after five hundred years, had it chosen the moment when he had been standing beneath to disintegrate? It was a statue depicting the baptism of Christ. The experience unnerved him. His feeling was he had to leave the city. He packed his books, his sketchbooks and his few clothes and drove east towards Umbria by way of Sansepolcro.

5

"Now you have to put on the blindfold," said Diane. Jared was sitting in the passenger seat of his own car. His wife, unusually, was at the wheel. She had re-touched her scarlet lipstick before setting out and her mouth had set in a hard line while she guided the vehicle out of the city towards the Tuscan countryside.

"I've already told you I'm not wearing a blindfold. Why do you always have to be so theatrical, Diane?"

"We agreed I need a place of my own. This is my sanctuary I'm taking you to. I don't want you to know where it is in case you ever get it into your head to turn up unannounced."

"You know I wouldn't do that."

"Can you at least close your eyes for five minutes then."

"I'll read that book you have in your bag. How's that?"

"Okay, if you promise not to look up."

Jared, accustomed to the capricious nature of his wife's often troubled mind and the appeasements it constantly demanded from him, pulled the book from Diane's bag.

"*Amare come Tradire*," he read. "Love as Betrayal." He flicked through its pages. "Was it you who underlined all these passages?"

"No. The book belongs to a friend of mine."

Jared read a paragraph and was dismayed.

"Isn't this rather melodramatic?"

"I find it helpful," said Diane, changing gears.

When after a couple of minutes, the car took a sharp bend, Jared looked up and saw the sign: Pèlago.

Today was his and Diane's wedding anniversary - eighteen years. One year less, Jared said, than it took for Ulysses to return to Penelope; one year less, Diane said, than it takes the moon to complete its cycle around the earth. Diane had given him as a gift an eighteenth-century papier-mâché Christ on the cross. Her intention, Jared inferred, was to mock him and his fascination with the Christ archetype.

"It's a gift, Jared. I thought you might like it. Why do you always have to read hidden meaning into everything?"

Jared looked at the blood-stained image through squinting eyes. "It's macabre. What am I supposed to do with it?"

When the papier-mâché Christ had been returned to its box Diane invited him to spend the weekend in the country. Jared had not initially been enthusiastic. Once again she was luring him away from his work. He had begun painting Mercy as Eve and was pleased with his lay-in. He had not yet told his wife about his new project.

Having arrived at the mill house, Diane showed him the paintings she was working on for her approaching exhibition. His eye alighted first on a picture of a nude woman - Diane - kneeling before a masked man. Jared was taken aback by its ill-disguised pornographic insinuations. He turned instead to a landscape.

"I like the harmony of this picture, even if the colour value is slightly falsified. It shows a new sophistication of touch and handling. You're not just pushing paint around for effect but going in with an eye to precision of form. At the studio I teach the students to use the darks to offset the light. Look at your shadows. You need to think about them more. What is the true colour of shadow?"

Jared moved on to another self-portrait - this time his wife had depicted herself as Leda. There was a contracted look of distress on her face as she did battle with a white tangled mass of swan's wings.

"Wasn't it Zeus' coupling with Leda that gave birth to

Clytemnestra and Helen? This was an act that brought about enormous destruction. Why did you paint yourself as Leda, Diane? Any reason? The abduction motif, is that it?"

"Leda was tricked into an act of love."

"Your Leda looks horrified by what's about to happen to her."

Diane loved her husband's painting and greatly esteemed his knowledge. At a dinner party in his apartment while Jared had been away she had in fact fallen in love with his paintings before meeting him. She had great confidence in the beguiling powers of her beauty and had no difficulty in flirting her way into Jared's imagination. The problem would arise when she told him about her husband and child. She gave him her diary to read while she went to Paris for a week. Jared had been impressed by her intelligence and moved by the pathos of her fate. Upon her return they had supper together in his flat. As Jared talked in English of her diary written in her native French tongue Diane twirled between finger and thumb her favourite flower, the yellow rose. Within the hour she had enticed Jared to unclasp the lion's head buckle around her waist. Jared was still hesitant in the weeks that followed. Being the son of a puritanical father, he felt himself in the grip of principles he found difficult to betray. They were married in America and spent their honeymoon in Salem; Diane however was still married to Tito in Italy. To divorce him was out of the question on the grounds that she simply could not bear to speak to him ever again.

"Be careful! There are lots of poisonous snakes lurking in the grass," said Diane triumphantly. Husband and wife followed a mud track along the stream's edge, not quite in step with each other, stumbling over tangled roots and stones embedded in the squelching soil. They sat down on the grass within sight of a waterfall. The black rocks over which the water tumbled and hissed were like sculptures of primitive female deities. The untrammelled fury of the waterfall made itself felt in the lower part of his body. Perched on every rock and in every crevice was an enormous colony of toads, almost all engaged in the act of copulation. An eerie occult knowledge seemed to reside in the primordial croaking noise they made.

Diane led Jared through nettles and briar, crossing the stream back and forth, balancing on makeshift wooden bridges and jutting slippery stones to get to what she called her resting place, an enclosed grassy verge close to the moving water. Jared fell asleep there. He woke up alone.

Embers were glowing in the fireplace and the flames of several candles were reflected in the varnish of the ceramics his wife had handpainted in another of her aborted bids for financial independence. Together with a few books they lined the wooden shelves of the dining room. Diane's psychotherapist had arrived for supper. Silvana was a heavy woman with dry wiry greying hair. She wore a surplus of ethnic jewellery and her clothes, wispy flowing fabrics, were an attempt to lighten the bulk of her frame. Her calloused crooked toes, exposed to view by the sandals she wore, did not meet Jared's approval. He looked at her from under his eyebrows, unwilling to give her the benefit of any doubt.

Jared was annoyed with his wife for springing this inappropriate surprise guest on him. It was after all their wedding anniversary. Dinner had begun in a reasonably civilised fashion but they had all drunk a considerable amount of red wine by the time the first candle had melted into its base.

"Even Plato conceded that Eros is the prime mover in the evolutionary imperative of every living thing on earth, Jared," said Silvana in her rasping deep-throated English.

"So we should all go around seducing whoever takes our fancy? Is that your philosophy, Silvana?"

"Shall I tell you why you're so in love with classical painters, Jared?"

"Oh please, Silvana. I'm sure it's not for the reasons I espouse every day at my school. Perhaps I just happen to recognise and appreciate beauty? But I'm sure you have a new angle on the subject. Come on, Silvana. Tell me why I love the old masters."

"You're in love with classical painters because they depict women either as prized possessions, passive slaves to man's desire or chaste virgins who arouse desire but are in no way capable of experiencing it. It was an art form which created an ideal of female passivity and a taboo of female sexuality."

"Balderdash, Silvana. You're wading out of your depth now. Have you actually ever looked at a Titian, a Rubens?"

"Those heroic rapes, you mean, in which the men seem to be enjoying a kind of blood-sport and the women strike fetching poses?"

"Oh Silvana, you're such a slave to fashion. What about the art you like? Van Gogh cut off his ear and sent it to a whore, Picasso stubbed out cigarettes on the flesh of his girlfriends. Is that what we should aspire to?"

"It would appear to me that nothing ever acquires new significance for you in the light of later experience. You won't let anything new be born in you. You're forcing Diane to express certain dark energies in their destructive forms because of the nature of your projections on her. Diane needs to regain possession of herself."

"Diane's mind has been dark since the day I met her," said Jared lowering his head.

"You've always insisted on creating the world in which I live, Jared, and ruling there with an iron fist," said Diane, clutching a flowered cushion to her breast. "I admit that when I met you I was guilty of projecting a father's role on to you. But I no longer need a father, Jared. And you won't see that. You'll never change."

"What are you saying, Diane?"

"I'm saying, you'll never change."

"Change!" he scoffed. "Why is change so all-important? You talk endlessly of change. What about fidelity, Diane? What about the abiding truths? Why are you so obsessed with forcing everything to undergo transformations? Perhaps the really important things don't change. Have you ever thought of that?"

The splashing thunder of the waterfall greeted Jared as, accompanied by his dog, he walked out into the vast crackling echo chamber of night. The darkness led his eye up to the bright web of stars overhead. He remembered what one of his students, a retired plastic surgeon, had said of the stars - that they were nothing but dead self-consuming lumps of matter. Nearby trees, awash in a heavy swell of shadow, were spellbinding in their luminous distinctness against the black sky. Jared began to feel himself alone in a place of origin. Hadn't he just begun a picture of Eve and been tempted by her?

So vividly aware of his movements, his physical presence was he that he began to feel like an intruder. Nothing in his present surroundings catered to his desires. He felt a resurgent dark tide well up at the back of his mind and was struck by the absence of colour around him. He had never really taken to charcoal drawings; it was colour - the fusion of translucent hand-ground pigment awash with the natural wonder of light - which struck all the major chords in his aesthetic sensibility. Slowly the images of the day began to take possession of his thoughts – the grotesque crucified Christ, the primordial orgy of copulating toads. As he looked out into the depths of the unlit night he realised the sun would be a long time in coming.

6

Julian Swallow, wearing brown dungarees, clicked his fingers as though in time to music going through his head. Costanza, to whose angular face blood easily rushed, was tall and willowy and would have looked the height of elegance in an expensive evening dress. Her long blonde hair was hidden today beneath a scarlet and gold headscarf. They were painting Rowan. As part of the advanced group, Julian and Costanza worked not in the main building on Borgo San Frediano but in another studio on Lungarno Serristori. Rowan was seated on a high chair in a large frescoed high-ceilinged room darkened by drapes and cloyed in thick oily smells overlooking the Arno. Jared, eagerly awaited, stopped by twice a week to give critiques.

"Nature has no lines," he was saying now. "Look in your mirror. If you work out the form in terms of light and shade you'll see the big shape much better. Get your darkest darks in first. Paint what you see in nature. You've given him sensual lips, Costanza, and Julian's giving him thin lips. What's going on? Are you two over-compensating for each other's oversights and exaggerations? Or are you both secretly painting yourselves?"

"Quite possibly, Jared," said Julian. "One does always tend to put something of oneself in every portrait. Also, I've always thought Costanza has a much better eye and feeling for colour than I do."

"Woman generally do. My wife often sees colours better than I do. Why is that do you think? Are women generally more sensitive? But then men are generally better draughtsmen."

"You can't have it both ways," smiled Julian disclosing the trickster gap between his two front teeth and waving his brush about in the air with a high-spirited flourish.

"And colour, getting the flesh tones right, is vital in capturing a person's character. I like your brush handling, Costanza. Are you finally loosening up? Is Rowan perhaps your muse? Do women have muses? Or is that a male thing?"

"Why shouldn't women have muses?" said Costanza, standing with her back to Rowan and looking at her painting in a small mirror.

"Oh, you just want everything men have for the sake of it," Jared teased her. "The muse is the man's anima - his idea of woman. Can men really be inspiring to women in the same way?"

"I don't see why not, Jared," said Julian, ever the diplomat.

"You have to understand, Rowan, that oil painting is alchemical," said Jared. "Look at our palette. We're using base metals together with an elixir - our medium - in order to create images. What, after all, are we doing if not trying to infuse matter with spirit? Another word for elixir is balsam which is the secret ingredient in our medium. In an old manuscript De Mayerne, the physician to Charles I, relates that Rubens dipped his brush in a mixture of aquaraggia and balsam to fuse his colours. And we have the gods for our flesh palette. We have white which is lead - Saturn, the great cosmic father; we have yellow ochre which is earth, Gaia; black is made of bone - Pluto, Hades. We've now moved down to the centre of the earth, the underworld kingdom. And how do we make all these transitions? With mercury. Vermilion is made from mercury. But mercury is also silver - quicksilver, *argentum vivum*, the living silver of the mirror which quickens the image into life. Mercury is the god of transformation. Is this alchemy or not? My quest is to find the elixir which will get the paint to flow and transform flesh into spirit. That was the genius of all the great masters. They summoned the soul up into their images."

Rowan thought about the quicksilver image on which his mind lately most dwelled - the image of Kira. Twice now he had dreamt about the lake which had assumed a magnetic quality in his imagination and to which he returned every evening just before sunset. She had not appeared again and so he had decided to seek her out at the dance school in via Ghibellina.

As he was crossing Ponte alle Grazie his attention was held by the sight of a fisherman on the bank of the Arno below. Rowan was transfixed by the tense quivering arc of the fishing line and the agitated smudge of living gold which appeared just beneath the surface of the water. The fisherman might have been battling with some leviathan so arduous was his struggle. He tugged the fish on the line over the stones onto the grassy verge and left it there to thrash about. For a while there was a tremendous death-defying fury in the fish as it slithered about on the grass. The fisherman flashed a triumphant smile up at the crowd that had now gathered on the bridge to watch him. With a sense of theatre he unhooked the fish and again looked up at the crowd. An angry woman told him to throw the fish back into the water. This though had clearly been his intention all along. The restoration of the fish to its natural element was greeted by a round of applause and the fisherman took a bow.

The dance school was next to an abandoned convent. He entered an office where a receptionist smiled expectantly at him from behind her desk. Rowan apologised for not speaking Italian very well and then invented a story about a female friend who was interested in resuming dance lessons. A dull incessant bass heartbeat pounded at the walls from the mysterious regions behind the reception area.

"A girl I met called Kira told me about this school," he explained.

The receptionist began looking in a drawer for some literature on the school. Rowan turned his attention to a framed black and white photograph on the wall. It featured two dancers, one of whom had long black hair and high severe cheek bones.

"Who's that woman?" he asked struck by her fierce beauty.

"Giuliana Cristalli. She studied with Martha Graham in New York and danced in her company for a while before coming to Florence. That's her in a dance called *Primitive Mysteries.*"

"Is she still alive?"

"No. She died in very tragic circumstances. She was one of the last people in Tuscany to be executed by the Nazis."

"What about the other dancer?"

"Her name is Bianca Monaco. She founded this school. That's her again," she said, pointing to another photo, "in a dance called *Errand into the Maze.*"

As a reaction was taking place in his blood to the name which held the key to the mystery of his birth he was aware of an influx of high-spirited voices. A door had opened somewhere in the recesses of the corridor leading out of the office. A troupe of female dancers appeared and filed past him. For a moment he expected to see Kira. However she was not among the exuberant train of girls who made their way out onto the street outside. A brittle elderly woman then appeared. Her grey hair was tied so tightly back into a bun that it pulled at her skin, emphasising her thin mouth.

"*Buongiorno*, Bianca," said the secretary.

"*Tutto bene*?" replied the woman. She looked at Rowan, studying him with an absence of emotional curiosity. He looked at her hands which appeared over-accustomed to gripping things tightly.

"My name is Rowan," he suddenly decided to say, in Italian. It was easier to act out of character in a foreign language. "I believe you knew my mother."

The pinched expression on her face bore the severity of an injunction. "Come with me," she said. He followed her out into a courtyard whose luminous green lawn blazed up with the solicitation of a secret laid bare. There was a long greenhouse through whose glass Rowan made out shocks of idyllic colour.

"In there nature is tricked. We have daffodils in October and roses in January. Let us sit down here," she said, pausing next to a wooden bench near a lemon tree. "I do not have much time today. You are without doubt interested in your mother. That, after all, I suppose is only natural."

"I'm not the most natural person in the world," said Rowan, trying to incite some affection in this potential oracle. The woman still had not smiled. He twirled the ring on his finger, a habit of his when he felt unsure of himself. "But I also wondered, seeing as you knew my mother, if that meant my mother danced too?"

"And what would that mean to you - if your mother was a dancer?"

"I rather like the idea."

"You English men, with your charm and flattery," she said with an undercurrent of bitterness. "Well, I'm sorry to have to disappoint you. Your mother was not a dancer. To be a dancer is to make sacrifices, sometimes of an unnatural nature. It is also to spend a great part of your life in front of a mirror. Often an unkind mirror. Before you know where you are there are two of you. Your body you begin to experience as a reflection in glass. Even when there is no glass you imagine glass. Yes, I did know your mother. Not as well as I should have known her. As I said to be a dancer is to make sacrifices. There was a man called Francis, English like you. He was infatuated with a very good friend of mine. But how difficult it is to tell stories."

"Is my father still alive?"

"That I have no way of knowing. Why do you ask me about your father?"

"But I did have a father? What I mean is, was my mother married?"

"Yes, she was married."

"And I was the legitimate son of that marriage?"

"Yes."

"What I don't understand is why I was given up for adoption."

"Your mother died in the flood."

"But I was given up for adoption before the flood."

Bianca Monaco looked at him sternly. "All of a sudden," she said, "everyone wants my memories. "Why not just live your life? Your mother has given you a healthy body, she's given you good looks, she's given you intelligence. What more do you want?"

"A heritage perhaps? A sense of being connected to a past."

"These things are only ideas. You have a heritage and you are connected to a past; you only lack the documents. I'm afraid I have to go now. I shall be away for a month or so. I will meet you when I get back." She delved into her purse and handed him a ticket. "At the amphitheatre in Fiesole."

7

"I wish you'd go back to painting me as Eve," said Mercy. She was speaking across the table to Jared at Cabiria, a bar in Piazza Santo Spirito where they had met up with some members of Jared's teaching staff.

"You don't enjoy posing as the Virgin?" asked Jared, relaxing back in his chair with his hands behind his head.

"It felt strange replacing your wife. Eve was more personal and thus more fulfilling."

"You're right. I should get back to my Eve before retouching the Virgin's hand."

"Do you still think the outline is too sharp on my cast drawing of Christ?" asked Mercy.

"Sharp lines draw too much attention to themselves, like ego. What's ego but a series of sharp lines which have yet to be softened? It's important to keep the eye moving around a drawing or painting. Focus is all about perceiving how different elements relate to one another. Only then do you truly see the large shape. You could soften your outlines still more. You don't suffer from ego, do you?"

"I don't have an ego, Jared," said Mercy, solemnly studying the reflection in her glass.

"Hey, Michael!" Jared called out across the table. "Did you hear what Mercy says? She says she doesn't have an ego."

"We all have our illusions," said Michael.

"But to get back to what I was saying," said Jared to Mercy, "think of Caravaggio. Caravaggio tended to keep his contours to the light relatively sharp while almost losing the shadow contour completely. The important thing is to search out variety in your treatment of edges and contours. What do you think, Daryl? You keep edges a lot sharper than I would. Not that I'm criticising you. Or perhaps I am criticising you. Daryl! Are you breaking one of my cardinal rules? You're my head assistant for god's sake."

"We actually have to make a move," said Daryl, carefully arranging a grey scarf around his neck and climbing apologetically to his feet. "Mercy and I are going out to dinner."

"Are you making moves on my muse?" asked Jared. "You know what happens when anyone makes moves on my muse? They hit the perilous siege."

"What's the perilous siege?" asked Daryl.

"The perilous siege is the seat at the Round Table which no one who isn't worthy can sit on. It's the Judas chair at the Last Supper. It rejects all those who aspire to what they haven't earned."

Daryl looked uneasy. His glasses had misted over in the smoky bar.

"Maybe Daryl and Mercy are going to become a couple," suggested Jared, watching them make their way through the maze of tables towards the exit.

"She won't fall for Daryl. He's too squeaky clean for her. She likes rebels, like Ingram," said Eliot. "Apparently she and Ingram went to a hot springs not far from Siena last week. While they were immersed in the thermal waters someone stole all their clothes, including Ingram's car keys. They were wearing nothing but towels when they stood by the side of the road at midnight trying to hitch a ride back to Florence."

"You mean they were both naked?" said Jared. "Hey look, speak of the devil! Here's Ingram. Ingram!" Jared called out, beckoning the blonde boy to join them. Ingram was wearing a kilt in the tartan of his clan.

"I hear you got naked with my muse," bantered Jared, not

noticing the grimace Ingram had thrown at Michael before sitting down. "I just want to warn you."

"Warn me about what?"

"Well, you're not exactly the most reliable person, Ingram," said Jared, knitting his brows and averting his eyes. "You never turn up at the studio. You spend all your time in these late-night drinking dens. Mercy is rather naive. I don't want you using her or leading her astray. She's also my muse, remember."

"I don't see what business it is of yours what Mercy and I do," said Ingram, looking down at the floor and its sullied confusion of wet footprints. "Anyway, if anyone's making Mercy's life here miserable it's Michael. He picks on her the whole time."

"What do you mean, he picks on her?"

"He's been rude to her since the day she arrived. Michael thinks he has the last word in ethical judgements," said Ingram.

"The Archangel Michael was the judger of souls."

"Here's Michael. Why don't you have it out with him," said Eliot as his friend appeared with another jug of sangria. Darkly bearded and long-haired, Michael offered as little of his face to the world as possible.

Ingram made a contemptuous face and pointedly ignored Michael.

"One thing you and Michael have in common is that you both have tattoos," said Jared. "Michael has a Celtic cross. Why don't you guys show each other your tattoos?"

Ingram rose to his feet and pulled his white lambswool sweater over his head and turned his naked back to Michael. The tattoo on his shoulder blade was of red flames licking at a broken circle.

"What's that, Ingram?" asked Jared. "A flaming sun?"

"It's a virility symbol from Borneo."

"Come on, Michael! Ingram's shown his colours, now it's your turn. Let's see your tattoo."

Michael removed his shirt disclosing the black cross on his muscular shoulder.

"Tell Ingram what your tattoo signifies."

"It's a Celtic cross - from the book of Kells."

"Is that a warrior symbol?"

"Warrior?" sneered Ingram, putting his jumper back on. "He picks on girls."

"Are you picking on girls?" bantered Jared.

"Have I ever told you what we do in Scotland on New Year's Eve, Jared?" asked Ingram.

"What do you do, Ingram?" asked Jared, smiling at Michael.

"We cut off the head of a live stag and take turns to wear it. And we dance around a fire and butt each other."

"Why do you do that?"

"To prove how virile and masculine we are," said Ingram drunkenly. "I'll tell you what, Jared; I challenge you to a drinking contest."

"Why don't you challenge me to a drinking contest?" asked Michael.

"Yeah, challenge Michael," said Eliot.

"Why don't you shut up," said Ingram. "What are you, some kind of lackey?"

"Hey guys, we're all friends here," said Jared.

"What exactly are you doing here, Ingram? You're not interested in art," said Michael.

"How the fuck do you know what I'm interested in?"

"Guys, guys!" shouted Jared. Everyone was shouting now. "Blessed are the peacemakers."

At that moment a group of musicians entered the bar and began playing what sounded like a Slavic folk song. Three dark-skinned girls sitting at another table got to their feet and began dancing, fanning out their long skirts and swooping back and forth between the tables. Wearing a blood red skirt, one of the girls tried to coax Jared into dancing but, becoming coy, he diverted her attention towards Michael who also refused the invitation. Ingram got to his feet and began drunkenly reeling around with the girls.

It had stopped raining when everyone tumbled out into the square. The virginal façade of Brunelleschi's church behind the square's trees seemed to emit a faint glow of its own. A few old women sat talking on the benches near the fountain. Ingram had climbed on a bicycle and was riding in tapering circles around Jared. "You're the greatest, Jared," he chanted. "Your school will go down in history. Keeping alive a noble tradition and all that. You will change the history of art. I could help you become even greater, Jared. I could crown you king of Scotland." Ingram lost control of the bike and crashed in a heap to the ground near the fountain. There was a cut on his leg when he staggered to his feet."Gonna head-butt you now, Jared," he said.

"Ingram! What's a head-butt?" asked Jared. His eyes too were bloodshot and a purple crust hardened the line of his mouth. "Is that some kind of pagan rite like prancing around with a freshly killed stag's head on your head?"

"I'll show you, Jared."

"Why don't you head-butt me?" challenged Michael, making a beckoning gesture with his hands. Ingram lowered his head like a bull and unsteadily charged. The two boys grappled in a confusion of parried blows. Jared looked on helplessly, unable to quite believe what was happening. He watched as Ingram bit Michael's hand and tore a clump of hair from his head. Michael, who up until now had held his superior force in check, responded with seething violence. He unleashed a series of punches before ramming Ingram's head against a parked car until the boy's body went limp and he collapsed with blood pouring from his nose.

"Gonna kill you," Ingram snarled when Michael released him, but he could hardly stand. Jared watched as two Italian men escorted him over to the steps of the church.

Michael, Eliot and Jared stood by the fountain. Jared noticed the moon had appeared between the clouds. When he looked over at the doors of the church Ingram was no longer to be seen. Michael washed his hand in the fountain, his blood staining and clouding the circulating water. A siren sounded and then a police car arrived in the square, its flashing light tinting the budding leaves of the young trees a sinister blue.

At four in the morning Michael and Jared were sitting on the floor in front of Jared's Descent from the Cross. "My marriage is over, Michael," Jared said, looking at his wife's portrait in the big painting. He swept his hair back and narrowed his eyes. "I've never thought about it in these final terms before but I've just had a kind of revelation looking at my picture. She's gone. I've lost her. What can one do when a marriage has broken down? We can't go on the way we are. We're both bad-tempered the whole time. I've tried, I really have. And then she gives me this macabre papier-mâché Christ. Practically throws it at me with a look of utter scorn on her face. I only ever wanted to be a painter. Maybe I should never have gotten married."

Jared looked at the reclining figure of Diane at the foot of the picture. Her head was cradled by a ministering angel in a gown of unworldly silver; her body had been swallowed up by the rich blue turbulence of folds in the robes she wore, her eyes were shut. In a strange way she too looked as though she had been crucified.

"Did I ever tell you how I came to paint this picture? My mother was involved in a serious car accident. So I made a vow. I promised that if she recovered I would paint a big picture in honour of the Virgin Mother. Is that odd? Of course, even when my mother recovered, I still had my doubts. I still don't know if I really believe. I need to understand what Christ means. This is what Diane cannot understand. Christ is the greatest archetype we have. Is it so wrong to want to understand what it means? I don't even know what my own picture means. Tonight it's taken on a whole new meaning. Tonight it seems like a lament to my dead wife. Before I always thought it was a poem to our love. How religious was your upbringing, Michael?"

"Pretty religious."

"And you believe in God? What about Heaven and Hell? Evil's always baffled me. Is it a force in its own right or is it more the good gone bad? Like tonight. Why did Ingram suddenly become a foe? He was like some little demon building up my ego. This is Holy Week. This happened in Holy Week. And then you were facing up to him like the angel who accompanies Christ into the wilderness."

"I love the way you've painted that hand, Jared. It's beautiful."

"I did that in one hour. It's Mercy's hand."

"Eve's hand."

"What do you think, shall I just leave it now?"

"Yeah. You shouldn't touch it."

"Okay, I won't touch it. I'll never touch that hand again," he said, looking at his wife's outstretched hand down at the bottom of the large canvas. Nestled in her open palm was a yellow rose.

8

Jared was out in the countryside near Pèlago, painting an interpretation of what he saw in front of his eyes - a foreground of parched grassland and shrub which ran down into a cluster of timeless grey buildings grouped around a church. There was an electrical pylon on the horizon which offended his eye and thus did not appear in his picture. Out in the open, exempt from social pressures, with a canvas in front of him, a palette and brush in his hand, he felt he was orchestrating the world around him into an order whose example he could follow. Nature was the great teacher - this it was that the old masters had taught him. Once Jared had established a symbiosis with the outlying landscape and entered into its rhythms he was able to assign a destiny to every stroke of pigment he laid down on his canvas. Not that he found painting easy. Nothing, in fact, could be further from the truth.

He fanned himself with his straw hat and studied the cloud formation - thin granulated fermentations of new life assuming forms as abstract as any modern painting. He could look at a landscape for hours - the shifting choreography of light and shade, the changing shapes of the clouds, the transfigurations of foliage and water as shadow swelled or sunlight solicited flux from the soil.

As he began to pack away his brushes, a breeze silvered the leaves of the olive trees on the slopes and he heard his dog yelping. It had got itself caught up in a thicket of thorns. It was Diane's dog. She had seen it in a market in the Cascine park. The vehemence of her desire for the puppy at any cost had taken him aback. He had given in. Now Diane had more or less abandoned the animal and it had become his responsibility.

While freeing the dog, the idea occurred to him to paint a crown of thorns on the head of his Christ. He began collecting thorns. When he had gathered up an armful he returned to his car. He had difficulty opening the trunk; it suddenly sprang up and struck him hard on the head. For a moment, Jared was stunned. Then he touched his crown; blood came off on his hands. He could feel it slowly trickling down the right side of his face.

"Michael and Eliot are being so mean to me," said Mercy. Daryl was painting her in his room at the Serristori studio having just returned with her from the Easter service.

"One thing I don't understand is why they don't seem to understand how inspiring you are as a model," said Daryl, dipping his paintbrush into the pot of sticky golden medium on his palette. "You've inspired Jared and also Julian's class and you'd think as artists they would at least appreciate that."

"I don't just want to be everyone's muse though. I want to be an artist myself. That's the whole reason I'm modelling here."

"I didn't mean that you're just a muse."

"Michael and Eliot don't take women seriously as artists. I also think they're jealous of my relationship with Jared."

"They've always been very possessive of Jared," said Daryl. "They're both a bit incensed about the way they're being treated by him at the moment."

"Michael and Eliot don't seem to like anyone. And they expect Jared to throw anyone they don't like out of the studio. I've heard them demonise several students to Jared, like Julian and Edward for example. And they're always really rude about other people's work. They'd be rude about their own work if someone else had done it."

"Jared's nerves are on edge at the moment. That's part of the problem. I don't think things are going very well with his wife. She told me recently - and this is strictly between you and me - that if he doesn't change she might have to leave him. She doesn't like Michael or Eliot. She was complaining that Jared was always out drinking with them."

"That would be dreadful if his wife left him," said Mercy.

Daryl watched her push out her breasts as she gathered up her hair in both hands behind her neck. "The studio could fall apart if that happened," he said.

"You should have seen the state of Ingram after Michael beat him up. I thought Michael was supposed to be a sensitive artist. Jared thinks Michael's mystical. I think he should go back to construction work in Chicago. In a way, I had the feeling that Michael beat up Ingram to get back at me."

"I heard Michael was protecting Jared. Ingram was so drunk he was going to hit Jared.Ingram had it coming to him. I think the guy is a bit of a jerk."

"I know what people think but it's not true. Me and Ingram were just friends. The whole relationship was entirely platonic. There's always so much gossip in this studio. You can't do any-thing without everyone knowing and then distorting it."

In the kitchen of the same apartment Eliot was saying to Michael, "I can't believe Jared got Mercy to expel Ingram. It's hard not to lose respect for him when he gets a girl to do his dirty work. And that girl has Jared twisted around her little finger. We'll be next. It's almost as if he's deliberately provoking us into leaving. Don't you feel that? Julian's his new favourite. When was the last time he actually said something complimentary about your work? He's always praising Julian and Costanza."

Michael was silent. He sat at the marble-topped table push-ing about breadcrumbs with a knife into the form of a cross when Jared let himself into the apartment, clutching a bottle of red wine.

"You won't guess what has happened. This is really going to amaze you, Michael. Look!" Having just sat down Jared got up again and, walking over to Michael, lifted a clump of his hair to reveal a gash in his scalp where stitches had been inserted. "Ingram ripped out your hair exactly where they've cut away mine to put in the stitches. Can you see the three little cross-shaped stitches. The cross again. And look there!" he said, nodding down towards the cross of breadcrumbs Michael had shaped on the table. "All this has happened Easter week. But it gets even stranger."

Michael went pale. Jared, who had been speaking of archangels and demons insistently since the fight and making allusions to himself as Christ, was beginning to unnerve him.

"Let me tell you the whole story," said Jared. "I was out painting a landscape when I heard the yelps of my dog. As you know, there's a dog on the plaque outside the studio. Wasn't there also a dog in *Faust*? Open the wine. Let's drink a toast. Happy Easter. It's the day of the Resurrection."

They all clinked glasses.

"My dog was all caught up in a thorn bush. While I was freeing him I thought, thorns; why not a crown of thorns? My Christ, as you know, does not have a crown of thorns. So I began breaking off branches. When I tried to open the trunk of the car it wouldn't budge until it sprung up and hit me on the side of the head. I had blood coming down my face and I was holding the crown of thorns. What do you make of that? Back in the studio, I opened the Bible at random and do you know what it said? *Think not that I am come to send peace on earth; I came not to send peace, but a sword.* You were my protector, Michael. Ingram wanted to strike me, but you directed him towards yourself." Jared clenched his fist and leaned forward. "I don't suppose either of you has read *Faust*? Is Mephistopheles behind everything? Have these strange things always been happening? Or is it just since Damien arrived at the studio? That thought occurred to me while I was in the hospital. Who is Damien really? Wasn't it Hermes who led the dead into the underworld? Perhaps Damien is Mercury come to announce a death - the death of my marriage."

II

Regnavi

9

"So if she hadn't been raped, I would not have been born, is that what you're saying?"

Vivienne Leyfield was sitting with her father's brother outside a coffee shop in Soho. The wet neon pleasure principle lights of central London outshone the fortune-telling stars; the moon was a dwindling presence above the gaseous sodium smog of the streetlights. Massive resources of energy could be felt throbbing through the invisible power lines of the metropolis.

Uncle Jack tugged at his beard and re-crossed his long spindly legs. A stranger to any social performance ethic his upper body sagged like someone who had run out of options. His young niece on the other hand had been taught that when options ran out new ones should be invented. "This woman," he continued in his deep baritone voice, "was already married when your father fell in love with her. And it was after she rejected him that he entered into the priesthood."

Vivienne's attention was constantly attracted to the bar or bistro across the road. She was intrigued by how much ice was being broken there. She felt excluded by the ease with which these party people communicated their affinity with the crackling surge of the night's current. And how fervently they all advertised their sense of belonging to the moment. These were the people who inhabited the nervous system of the city's metabolism, the people who were carrying the viruses of the future. Her uncle in comparison seemed a throwback to some virtually extinct world of the past. She had not been prepared for an emotional experience tonight; she had contemplated the prospect of meeting with her bohemian uncle with reluctance, and until the last minute she had considered inventing an excuse to postpone the encounter. The evening had taken a sharp turn towards more taxing realms the moment she had mentioned her imminent departure for Florence.

"Which means you're following in your father's footsteps," her uncle had said. "But then you always have been daddy's girl. How is your mother?"

"She's fine. She's taken up meditation."

"I've always thought you should make more effort with your mother. You're severe on her because you're impressed by intellect and she's not intellectual."

"I get impatient with women who are secretly happy to play the victim."

"What about your little caper at Oxford. You were quite happy to play the victim then. I heard you ended up blaming the don for your prank."

It had been her friend Siobhan's idea, conceived after one too many glasses of champagne. They had entered the study of the dowdy old don together, giggling. Siobhan had quickly slipped out of her skirt and t-shirt and walked slowly to the man's desk in her favourite black push-up-and-plunge bra and lacy black knickers. They were both very drunk. The caper misfired when the don refused to follow their script or even see the funny side of it. Siobhan, already having graduated with a humiliating 2:1, had fled to Florence; Vivienne, wearied by the social and intellectual pressures of Oxford, had decided to abandon ship before she could be sent down.

"What you did wasn't by any chance an unconscious way of getting back at your father?"

"How do you mean?"

"A university professor is obviously a paternal figurehead. He represents authority. You tried to humiliate one. Doesn't it speak for itself? You were calling to account the entire structure you've been born into, flaunting your contempt for it."

"Let me get this straight," she said now. "Dad was in love with this woman in Florence but she was married and then raped, by whom we're not quite sure? You're not, I take it, insinuating Dad was involved?"

"What I'm saying is the rape of this woman did affect your father deeply. One might almost say it led him into the priesthood. Of course that didn't last long because PJ's eye will insist on roving."

"He fell in love with Mum."

"And was defrocked. After which you were born. Rape in mythology is often the prerequisite for the activating of fate."

"I'm not sure I believe in fate, Uncle Jack, but I have always felt drawn to Florence," said Vivienne, covering with her hand the sensual affluence of her bee-stung lips.

Vivienne stood in a square of light. It fell down from the high windows of the deconsecrated former church. She looked at a plaster cast representation of the *Pietà*. The male in a state of spiritual passivity awaiting the new idea, ministered by the forgiving female. But all the discoloured statuary, with its exemplary line, stared back at her with a forsaken outmoded air. This was her first day in Florence and she felt weightlessly unanchored, more conscious of the unarticulated silent spaces of her mind. Her most pressing imperative was to hold herself in check, maintain her self-possession. To imagine herself betraying externally the secret of what she felt, the close proximity of her vulnerability, was to offer up a binding sacrifice to all that was ungovernable and treacherous in her nature - to give it not only credence but causality.

Siobhan, in a black pvc mini skirt and a white cashmere sweater, opened the splintered wooden door of the cast room onto the street. Two boys were standing idly by the road while a raucous procession of traffic vomited out exhaust fumes into the direct sunlight of the late afternoon in April.

"This is Algernon Duff, Algie to his friends," Siobhan said, presenting to Vivienne a young man wearing a grimy cowboy hat. His greeting, delivered in a pleased piping Irish accent, was a performance in itself and struck Vivienne as almost vaudeville in its self-regarding sentimental showmanship. "He's a classicist who can't read a word of either Greek or Latin. You know how I just adore frauds. And this is Andrew Hayward-Salt." Andrew, shorter and coyly dressed in a tweed jacket, held himself very erect and firmly gripped Vivienne's outstretched hand. A gossamer sheen of sweat waxed his face.

"So this is the famous Archangel Raphael?" she said nodding up at the marble plaque under which students were filing out of the building. "Jared was telling me about him earlier."

"The Archangel Raphael was the healing angel," said Andrew eagerly. "He brought back sight to the blind. Is that not appropriate? What, if not that, is Jared trying to do here? Our ability to see has been destroyed by the modern emphasis on flitting frivolously from one image to another."

"Florence strikes me as the ideal place for those unwilling to contemplate anything which offends the eye."

"To my mind modern art offends the eye. The modern world offends the eye. Isn't that why we're all drawn to Florence? To experience a more spiritual vision of life?"

"That's not why I've come to Florence. I've come to rape and pillage,' said Vivienne, sending herself up with elaborate archings of eyebrow and insolent flashings of teeth. Andrew laughed politely.

They were walking side by side a few feet behind Siobhan and Algernon. Soon they reached the river. On the other side of the water, beyond the distant thunder of the weir, the chalky white church of Ognissanti caught Vivienne's eye and she was ashamed she did not know its name.

"I'm actually rather worried about our gardener," said Andrew. "You see, there was a dreadful storm just before I left for Florence and many of the trees on our large estate in Kent were literally uprooted by the force of the wind. One of them fell on our gardener who had to be taken to hospital."

"Well, you know nature," Vivienne said, "always biting the hand that feeds."

The over-earnest Andrew and his fallow long-winded anecdotes provided Vivienne with the perfect foil for the easy irreverent slingshots of her wit. She was passing through a phase in her life where she almost purposefully renounced the dialectics of an inner register. In her book, flippancy and satire were just as likely to move her to within reach of what she wanted as soul-searching or political forums and were certainly more fun. More often than not she took pride in recognising the pliant insincerities of her performances. These, she reasoned, could only extend her resources and thus make her more interesting. Her self, if such a tethered ministrating oracle existed, would always be there; why draw attention to it when there were so many other qualities she might by imitating make her own?

"He was pitifully contrite afterwards," Algernon Duff was assuring Siobhan up ahead. "It's easy to imagine - a few harsh drunken words, a spear enticingly at hand...and then poor distraught Alexander was wailing inconsolably on the floor beside the dead body of his beloved Cleitus."

"Like most males he couldn't take criticism?" suggested Siobhan.

Algernon threw his head back and emitted an appreciative chuckle. "By the way, there's an update on the defection of Michael and Eliot. Apparently they jettisoned the studio drill and Mercy's cherished hiking boots in the Arno before catching a flight back to Chicago."

"They called me a gap girl. I wasn't here for the same noble reasons they were. They always boasted of their poverty as if it's somehow clever to come from the richest country in the world and be poor."

Algernon tossed back his head and once again there emerged the falsetto chuckle.

The two girls refused to join Algernon and Andrew for a drink and made their way to Piazza della Signoria where a wind flung spray from the Neptune fountain into their faces. They sat down on the steps of Palazzo Vecchio with the sweep of the piazza laying naked before them like an empty stage.

"So?" said Siobhan. "Are you going to like it here?"

"I absolutely adore it already."

"Do you see what I mean though about it being a kind of Euro-Disney Renaissance theme park? One would only need to dress up some of the locals in medieval costume and pay them to poke pigs to the market. Sometimes one can almost even seduce oneself into pretending that all the values represented here still have some bearing on the way one might live one's life. But then the streets are bristling with the usual eurotrash lemmings and it becomes quite clear the divine comedy consists not in how you choose to confess your sins but in how you choose to advertise them. Florence is the ideal refuge for those who have no wish whatsoever to change- the unyielding sanctity with which it beholds its own glorious past acting as a kind of moral support to any personal reluctance to wear some new clothes."

10

The Range Rover pulled off the brightly lit companionship of the autostrada and its headlights burnt into the sodden repository of darkness of a lonely country lane. Damien's house was completely isolated and reached by way of a long winding dirt track. It stood on the summit of a hill overlooking a sweep of olive groves and was engirdled by more hills. The ground clung to her feet as Vivienne made a dash through the rain to the house. The front door opened into the living room, darkened by its low wooden beams. A large pile of ash lay attracting attention in the fireplace and the room smelt vaguely of charred bracken and black smoke. Damien, helping Mercy off with her unisex coat, drew attention to the wrought iron Adam and Eve motif on the fireplace over which hung a pair of stag's horns.

"You ought to feel at home here," he told Mercy. "Look, there's your prototype."

The American girl's casual sporty attire - jeans, hiking boots and a nondescript sweater - made Vivienne feel overdressed in her short skirt, black tights and low-cut top.

Damien conducted his two guests on a tour of the house. Room after room met Vivienne's scrutiny with a fastidious reluctance to disclose its history. The stairs did not creak though the rooms upstairs all produced a slight echo which seemed to steal from her what she said and reiterate it in another, more desolate realm. There were three bedrooms. He did not show the girls his own.

"Now that we're on neutral turf, tell me the truth," said

Damien at dinner which had been provided by a catering service. "Don't you sometimes both feel at the atelier as though you belong to some spellbound religious sect?"

"I want to learn how to paint and Jared is a wonderful teacher," said Mercy with her arms folded rigidly over her breast.

"But are you free to think what you like?" He refilled her glass with red wine despite her earlier refusal of a second glass.

"I don't understand what you mean. Of course I'm free to think what I want. How could anyone stop me from thinking my own thoughts?"

"So Jared hasn't brainwashed you yet?" Rarely was there not an amused playful light in Damien's dark eyes. "There's no question he means well but his idea of beauty, if I may say so, is not terribly far-sighted. Byzantine icons are very beautiful as are Navajo sand paintings but of course they weren't chiaroscuroed and so don't get the royal seal of approval. Isn't this whole chiaroscuro obsession a bit of a charlatan trick?"

"I feel a great affinity with Jared," said Mercy. "I admire him for what he's trying to do. He cares about beauty and has a vision of how life might be improved. Most men I know just accept the way things are and set out to exploit this treadmill for their own gain."

A window gusted open. The flames of the red candles dripping wax onto the white tablecloth became agitated as a breath of the sodden world outside entered the house. Damien got up to close it.

"In some circles," he said, returning to the table with flecks of rain in his hair, "Jared's school is thought of as a healing place. He is, after all, the custodian of a church, albeit a deconsecrated church. I know people in England whose floundering children found a sense of self-worth during the three years they spent at Jared's studio. In fact, the parents of Ingram Perth-Campbell were hoping Jared could help free him of his demons. But, by all accounts, his demons have taken an even greater hold. And now Jared has banished him. The studio has failed him. Will you allow me to be mystical for a moment?" he said, leaning forward closer to the flame of a candle. "It's my belief that the *genius loci* has been profaned by a violation which took place in the building in 1966. And the arrival of someone connected to that event has triggered those dark psychic energies. Have either of you heard of the great flood which struck Florence in 1966? I only missed that ferocious onslaught of female nature by three days."

"Why was it female?" asked Vivienne. "Or do you simply blame all things destructive on women?"

"Water is female - in its drowning properties and primeval fury no less than in its baptisms, irrigations and tidal rhythms. Perhaps you don't understand this because you are not, at least yet, a very womanly female."

"How on earth would you know what kind of female I am?" asked Vivienne, indignant.

"Don't get me wrong; I actually find that very attractive. Womanly females tend to be rather suffocating and conventional. Tampering with nature, after all, is how we've evolved as a race."

"You're turning an insult into a compliment?"

"Or, as an alchemist might have it, the nigredo into the albedo," he smiled, pausing to knock ash off his cigarette. "But did you know that water symbolises the entrance to the underworld? That perhaps explains why supernatural powers are often perceived in the vicinity of underground springs and wells. By water, spirits return to take what is their due. This is why in early Christian times when Christianity was still very much under the influence of pagan beliefs the crypt of a church was flooded with water. The crypt, you see, is where the sacred mysteries would take place. It was also the place of baptism. The violation I spoke of took place in the crypt of the school. Do you know it's suddenly dawned on me that I may once have known a member of your family?"

"Which member of my family?" asked Vivienne, leaning back in her chair.

"PJ he was known as. I never did find out what his first name actually was. PJ Leyfield."

"Peter John," supplied Vivienne. "He's my father."

"I thought so. I met him here in Florence. Actually, in those days, your father was something of a rake."

"I've never heard anything so preposterous in my life. My father was a priest."

"Oh, so that's what he did next; I had always wondered. You see, we lost touch after Florence."

Vivienne had risen furiously to her feet with the intention of leaving, until she remembered she was isolated in the middle of the Tuscan countryside.

"It is however interesting that you and not your father have returned to the scene of the crime," said Damien.

The knock on the door struck her as being uncommonly violent and loud. Vivienne groped for the bedside lamp. She saw the silhouette of Damien Sparks. He hesitated between the world of light behind him and the world of darkness before him. After floundering about in the dark like a drowning swimmer, she succeeded in making contact with the light switch. At that moment light struck her as a kind of miracle. She felt her entire body complete a transition as it adjusted itself to being able to see.

"I just wanted to apologise for what happened tonight. I really didn't mean to be..."

"Rude?"

He was edging his way by slow degrees towards the intimate part of the room - the bed in which Vivienne lay with the covers pulled up to her neck. She shifted beneath the sheets and the displacement of folds elicited a faint smell of perfume.

"Would you agree that there's a secret symbolic language which speaks through all things?" he said. His outline had acquired a faint luminosity from some light of the night outside.

"A kind of sign language in which both animate and inanimate objects partake. And that one of our challenges in life is to evolve our understanding of the correspondence between inner and outer worlds. For example, a thought too long brooded on can become an entity in its own right. An act of separation takes place in which the thought takes on agency in the outside world. You see it's my belief that you're held captive by some emotional remembrance of things past."

"A friend of mine died," said Vivienne with a note of aggression, reaching for her cigarettes.

"A boyfriend?"

"Well, he was a boy and he was a friend, but we never slept together, if that's what you mean. I met him while I was travelling in India. He was dying of AIDS. The proximity of death made him seem very wise. We had long talks on a beach near Madras. He loved trees. I had always scorned nature loving as corny insincere new age claptrap. I love London and miss it. And yet he made me feel the beauty of things with roots which push down under the earth. The night he died - I had returned to England by then - I had a dream in which I met him on a beach and he gave me a shell. The next day I found an almost identical shell on this beach in Devon where I was staying."

"That's very interesting. Jared and I often discuss synchronicity. In fact, I'm carrying out a kind of experiment on the subject. I see you're sceptical. How about if we test synchronicity? Give me a word. And I guarantee events affiliated with the word will follow."

"Cave," she said.

"Cave? That's good."

"I really do need to get some sleep."

"How about a kiss before I go to bed?"

Vivienne allowed him to kiss her on the cheek.

A few days later, Damien appeared as she was leaving the studio. He was standing by the bas- relief of Tobias and the Archangel Raphael. He held a small box.

"I hope you haven't come to propose to me," said Vivienne seeking to laugh off the uneasiness she felt.

He opened the lid. Inside was a dead scorpion brocaded with gold leaf.

"Why would you do that?"

"The alchemists used the scorpion as an agent to expunge poison. You don't find it beautiful?"

No," she said, covering her eyes with her hands.

"By the way, do you remember our discussion about synchronicity and how you came up with the word cave? Well, I received an email yesterday. An uncle of mine called Nigel Cave died on the morning after we had our conversation. But you mustn't think you killed him. You actually did him a huge favour. He was in terrible pain and probably his death came as a godsend at the end. But you see what I mean?"

11

In the kitchen, Rachel stirred spinach simmering on the hob in preparation for the guests soon to arrive. Rowan was browsing through a book of photographs of both the second world war years in Florence and the 1966 flood. He gazed at black and white images of Hitler and Mussolini on the balcony of Palazzo Vecchio; of Florence's famous sculptures hidden inside corrugated iron sheds; of the removal of the Gates of Paradise from the Baptistery; of the debris of the medieval district near Ponte Vecchio, an excavation site of shards and broken walls, after the bridges had been destroyed by the retreating Germans.

He then arrived at the photographs of the flood that had taken the life of his mother. He wondered in what part of the city his mother had died, whether he had ever walked over the exact spot where she had thought her last thought. He had sometimes been able to produce a fleeting vision of what his mother looked like; it stole upon him in moments of tiredness or distraction like something not quite of this world, more a feeling than an arrested image.

"I was looking at that book this morning," said Rachel. "Did you know the force of the water tore down the Gates of Paradise? It's a miracle more people didn't die."

The slamming shut of car doors made the windows rattle in their frames. "Sounds like Jared and his wife have arrived," said Rowan.

The path of the sun blazed over clusters of spring flowers whose scent drew the women over to its source. Jared and

Rowan wandered off towards a small lemon grove. "This is what has always been denied Diane and me," said Jared, looking up at the abbey through an aisle of arching branches. "A home in the country. It's a lovely house, don't you find? Fate works in strange ways. I remember when Tim and Rachel were more or less in the same situation as Diane and me - cooped up in a small flat in the city. Now here they are in this beautiful old farmhouse with its low wooden beams, original brick floors and fireplaces while I'm still in my rented apartment in the city. Not that I'm complaining. I couldn't really live way out here in the country when I've got the studio to run. Diane already had a child when I met her. Do you think everything is decided right from the beginning? We had the responsibility of a child before we even got to know each other properly. Everyone here seems very happy, don't they? There's a real family atmosphere. Tim playing games with his children, Rachel helping little Roland with his homework. And even when he broke that old nineteenth-century wooden crib she kept very calm. In my home, Diane would have erupted and there would have been a huge scene."

Rowan got a lift back to Florence in Jared's car, squeezing between Julian and Costanza in the back seat. Jared could not resist making a joke.

"Is Rowan coming between you two? Might you not have a rival, Julian? You should see the portrait Costanza has painted of Rowan," he said to his wife in the front seat. "She's made him look as dashing as Lord Byron."

"I'm all for Costanza expressing herself," said Julian.

"Equality between the sexes, right?"

"Perhaps Rowan is as dashing as Lord Byron," said Diane, looking up at the rear-view mirror and catching Rowan's eye in its unpolished glass. Rowan smiled back nervously, aware that Jared too was looking at him in the same mirror.

"What did you make of Tim's sons and daughters, Julian?" said Jared.

"They're very tall," said Julian.

"Do you know, Julian, sometimes I think Jared resents me because I have not given him a son."

Jared frowned at his wife. "I'm happy with my daughters; why would I need a son?" he said. "What about you, Julian? Can you imagine yourself with a son?"

"At the moment I have enough on my plate learning to paint portraits," said Julian.

"I don't want a son. Sons eventually set themselves up as rivals to their father. I want daughters who will worship me," said Rowan, in jest.

"There you go. It's true sons do want to steal their father's privileges. Eventually the son will step into his father's shoes. It's like the story in *The Golden Bough*. You know, the priest whose role was always up for grabs to anyone who succeeded in tearing a bough from the tree the extant priest guarded. The king is dead, long live the king. Maybe it's just as well I don't have a son."

"Only prodigal sons," said Diane. "Like Michael and Eliot."

At Julian's suggestion, they stopped off at San Miniato to hear the monks chanting. Inside the church they climbed up to the choir to get a better view of the large mosaic of Christ.

"Once a year, in September," Jared said, "the rays of the setting sun enter through one of the clerestory windows and shroud the left foot of Christ in a blaze of gold. The idea is that Christ's foot is being healed every year. Look at the at the four Evangelists in the mosaic. There's John accompanied by the eagle, Mark accompanied by the lion, Matthew by the winged human and Luke by the ox. Now look at the lectern. What do you see, Rowan?"

"The lion, the human and the eagle."

"But no ox. When the priest climbs the pulpit he becomes the ox - the Christ who shed His blood for humanity. Now perhaps you see just how pagan this church is. The bull, which astrologically we can say is the ox, being the divinity of the old Mithraic cult. Taurus is the voice, which is the priest's role, to deliver the Word. Here it's the symbol of Christ the Logos. If you look on either side of you, you'll see two fish, the symbol of Pisces. Pisces is the feet. Hence the healing light on Christ's foot. Through Taurus the Word we descend into matter, through Pisces we ascend into spirit."

"I'm a Pisces," said Rowan.

"And aren't you a Taurus, Jared?" said Julian.

Jared nodded.

"I didn't know Taurus was related to the voice," said Diane.

"You mean it explains why I'm so talkative," said Jared. "Do you believe in astrology, Julian?"

"I don't see any reason not to believe in it."

They turned their backs on the mosaic of Christ and retraced their steps back to the marble zodiac on the floor.

"The celestial wheel," said Jared.

"Or the wheel of fortune," said Julian.

"I suppose you're right. It is a wheel of fortune. But what does it all mean? What do you think, Julian? Is this a Christian church or a pagan temple of blood sacrifice?"

"Almost all early churches were built on the sites of pagan temples, Jared," said Julian. "Life is all about layers."

"Is that the onion theory?"

"You can't make something go away just by building on it just as you can't make something go away by not believing in it."

Rowan wandered down the right aisle and descended into the crypt where several people were praying before the altar. He sat down amidst the slender columns, the honeycomb vaulting and the bright vanishing frescoes with all the prayer candles flickering shadows over the walls. The translucent chant of the Benedictine monks ascended from below as lightly and evanescently as the flight of a newly metamorphosised butterfly. Rowan's thoughts again turned to his mother and her death until it seemed, in the dark crypt, that the ghostly echoing chant of the monks was for her.

Jared dropped him off at Santa Croce and Rowan caught a bus up to Fiesole as the sun was setting. The bus turned a corner and the sweep of cypresses on the terraces beneath the town were all awash in liquid gold. Man-made Florence down in the valley, a clutter of tiny boxes draped in shadow, looked belittled in the face of this blaze of transfigured nature.

Lit beautifully by footlights, the Roman amphitheatre was half-full when Rowan entered. The empty stage below was a simple black platform with white geometric lines drawn over it. Rowan looked up at the moon and felt himself inch closer to the part of his mind where revelation might occur. He waited for Bianca Monaco who, as the seats around him began filling up, showed no sign of arriving. From his seat he could see the outline of the neighbouring hills and all at once life seemed very ancient to him. No doubt individuals who had made sacrifices to grain goddesses had sat on this same stone bench and looked out at these same hills. As his mind, like a stuttering flame, reached back into the darkness of the past he felt a sense of well-being take hold of him.

For a while the only lighting was faint and discontinuous, often illuminating a void into which a body threw itself and then vanished again. Whenever a dancer was caught in the spotlight she moved with the fluidity of an image on water. A deep visceral grinding of cellos and violins, a gathering sweep of strings strained towards an epiphany which never quite arrived. One female dancer in particular caught Rowan's eye. She appeared in white and slowly, trance-like, repeated a sequence of movements within a closed and yet self-renewing circle.

Rowan felt elated when the performance was over. He had all but forgotten Bianca Monaco's failure to materialise.

12

Mercy stood naked on the podium while Jared unfurled the rhythms of her curves in filaments of light and residues of shadow. They were listening to Monteverdi's *Vespro della Beata Virgine* and the voices of the sopranos swirled overhead among the motes in the darkening high-ceilinged room. At this time of the day the light rippled over Mercy with a lingering tenderness. Jared wondered, as his eye moved from the delicate small blue veins in Mercy's thighs to the erect rose-bud appeal of her nipples, if the naked body of a beautiful girl was the ultimate reward sought by the male in all his quests and conflicts or if its allure was simply a stunningly clever biological trick. Was Mercy, as the personification of awakening female beauty, the end of all longing, or was she instead a siren designed to lead the male astray?

"Where do you think temptation leads us, Mercy? *Lead us not into temptation...* but where does temptation then lead us? Is giving way to temptation always bad, do you think?"

Mercy relaxed her outstretched right arm in which she held the apple and Jared saw the shadow it cast beneath her breasts shift slightly downwards. "The Bible says that an act committed in the mind is the same as an act committed by the body," she said. Mercy had a habit of replying to questions warily, as if on trial before a harsh and hair-splitting jury - this, so Jared deduced, was her God, listening in at all times to everything she said, ready to reprimand her for the slightest slip of the tongue. He wondered how intelligent, how evolved a response this was to life. Were we merely here then to stand trial every day of our lives, to be tripped up by some unrelenting prosecution counsel?

"But is that really true? That's a very literal way of reading things." Jared strode up to his canvas again, a hair's breadth away from the naked Mercy offering her fruit. Behind the pungent smell of turpentine and pigment he was aware again of the elusively porous fragrance on her skin and hair. "Perhaps," he said, mixing a dash of vermilion with lead white on his palette, "our imagination is a kind of purgatory where it's okay to experience the weaknesses of our nature and where we don't have to inflict them on the world at large?"

"All evil though is brewed in the imagination."

"Are you talking from personal experience?" asked Jared, pointing at her in mock accusation with his brush.

"I think there's probably a big difference in the way men and women experience temptation. I think temptation is something men read into women and women play with. Sometimes a woman will deliberately tempt a male in order to make herself feel more attractive."

"But where does temptation lead us? Does temptation always belong to the weaker part of our nature and is it how we're lured away from our higher self, or can succumbing to temptation sometimes be a positive act? A means of acquiring knowledge? What was the real significance of what happened in the Garden of Eden? What does Eve think? Is temptation a desire for knowledge?"

"I think if anything tempted me to the point of obsession it'd be wrong not to yield. But I know I could never be tempted by anything bad."

"Yielding to temptation is also a surrender," he said, lowering his eyes to his palette. "It's often the moment in which we abandon our moral sense to indulge our animal nature. Christianity has always sought to elevate the mind or spirit, but has it ever really dealt with the body? Are all our bodily appetites really so bad that we have to suffer guilt for succumbing to them? Maybe the old pagan religions were wiser when it came to the body. You see, Mercy, I had a very strict upbringing. I was taught to live in my mind and I've suffered as a result. What kind of upbringing did you have? Are your parents born-agains as well?"

"My parents are very open-minded. They've never taught me to feel ashamed about anything. Just the opposite."

Shadow had begun to creep forth from the occluded areas of Mercy's body, emphasising contours but blurring detail. Looking at his picture now Jared realised he was having problems with the design of the pose. On his canvas her arms had assumed the vaguely menacing juxtaposition of scissors about to snap shut. Having spent ten years guiding his students away from the danger of creating sharp edges - lines do not exist in nature and thus should be blurred in subordination to the shape as a whole - he himself had lapsed into the cardinal sin. There was menace in the poise of Mercy's arms.

"But to get back to the Garden of Eden, it's interesting that temptation and knowledge are so inextricably entwined. What do you think of the Islamic fundamentalists who insist on women wearing veils and not receiving any kind of formal education? Aren't they trying to reverse what happened in the Garden of Eden? To cover a woman's face would imply that temptation enters a man through the eyes and that intellectual knowledge in a woman is dangerous."

"I think men are frightened of a woman's powers."

"Perhaps women are frightened of their own powers though. Have you thought of that? But by eating the fruit of knowledge Adam and Eve's eyes were opened – that's what it says in the Bible. Isn't that interesting because what am I trying to do here but open people's eyes? What though do you think is the significance of the snake? Someone once said that maybe Eve was seduced by the snake. That she lost her maidenhead to the snake and so poor old Adam was not only cuckolded but had to suffer the consequences of a crime he did not even commit."

"Talking about the snake again, Jared?" said Damien Sparks,

suddenly appearing in the room. "You know, of course, the snake was a symbol of wisdom and renewal in ancient cultures?" Catching a glimpse of the naked Mercy he made a point of averting his eyes but the girl was already indignant. She jumped down from the model stand, made towards the door, changed her mind, hesitated in the middle of the room and, like a wood nymph pursued by a lusty god, scampered behind Jared's easel.

"Damien! Have you come to ogle my model?"

"I only popped in to get my car keys back. I lent them to Mercy."

Mercy's dramatic flight had made a compelling spectacle of her nakedness and perhaps also revealed the governing imperative of her vanity - to arouse desire only to immediately and with a show of indignation repel it. Had she once again provided an insight into the nature of Eve as an archetype? And yes, she did tempt him. Not that he would ever act; it was only in imagination that she lured him into betraying his wife; but then what had the girl earlier said? That a deed performed in imagination is tantamount to the act itself - in which case he had been unfaithful to Diane.

When Damien had thought it better to leave, Jared told her to lift her arm a little higher and then, no longer able to ignore the brooding resentment with which she looked down at him, asked her what was troubling her.

"Damien entering like that has made me feel uncomfortable. He had no right to just walk in. There's a difference between being painted nude and being scrutinised nude."

"He was ogling you? I'm sure he got a much better of view of you because you ran across the room naked and hid behind my easel. Could you not have just covered yourself up? I've heard it said that you're jealous because all of a sudden Damien is taking more interest in Vivienne. This isn't a case of sour grapes, is it Mercy?"

Mercy looked horrified. She maintained the pose but all her joints went stiff. "I don't believe you even said that, Jared. Damien is old enough to be my father."

"Come to that so am I, Mercy."

"Why is everyone so against me? Michael had this conspiracy thing going against me for absolutely no reason. Now you are taking sides against me."

"No one is taking sides," said Jared, with a deep sigh. "Let's take a break."

Jared carried on adding paint to his picture while Mercy, having slipped into a robe, walked over to his painting of the blind man. She was wearing today a ring with a glittering black stone. Jared had never seen it before. When she put her hand to her forehead he had a vision of her with a glittering jet-black eye.

"By the way," he said, with a new note of wariness in his tone, "what's this story about Damien giving you some money?"

"Nothing stays a secret in this studio. I'm going to pay it back as soon as I can. I needed some money for personal reasons."

"Are you not earning enough modelling? You must be making a fair bit now. Why didn't you come to me?"

"You've already been so good to me, Jared. You're letting me study here for free; you're letting me live at Serristori rent-free. I'm becoming a burden. I bet you'll even find a model with more beautiful breasts than mine and paint over me," she said.

13

Jared arrived late to the opening of Diane's exhibition. She threw him a reproachful glance and carried on talking to Tim and Rachel Garnett. Jared noticed that underneath each painting was a poem written in Italian. He looked at one blankly, reading words without taking in their meaning. The poem was beneath the picture of his wife kneeling naked at the feet of a masked man.

"What are these poems?" he asked Diane. "Did you write them?"

"Some I wrote and some were written by Angelo d'Alba, a friend of mine."

"And what does your angel of the dawn do apart from writing poetry?"

"He's an *ufficiale guidiziario.*"

"You mean he's a bailiff. He takes away other people's property," said Jared. When he saw Silvana approaching he walked off to get another glass of wine.

"You still haven't found a way out of the labyrinth, I take it," said Silvana.

Diane had a pained look on her face. She was looking at her portrait of her elder daughter Francesca. Somewhere along the line she had lost the likeness. At times while painting her daughter, she had found herself envying the girl's nubile taut body and wondered if her envy hadn't found its way onto the canvas. The portrait now seemed to mock her attempt to revive her younger self.

Diane had spent endless hours in therapy of one kind or another. She had listened to her problems being discussed in terms of astrological configurations, chakra blockages, ancestral curses, unconscious compensations, splits between feeling and thinking functions and, more often than not, a father fixation. She had spent an entire year writing down her dreams and had painted some of their images into her pictures.

"I have a question for you two girls," she said, ignoring Silvana and instead turning to Vivienne and Mercy who were standing close by. "Can we defy destiny?"

"I'm not quite sure that I know what you mean by destiny," said Vivienne. "Since I've arrived in Florence everyone seems to be talking about this thing called destiny. It all sounds kind of outdated to me, like referring experience to the antics of the Greek gods."

"Destiny as I understand it is God's will," said Mercy.

"So if I defy destiny I am defying God's will?" said Diane.

"But how can a woman believe in a male god, Mercy?" asked Silvana. "And more important, how can a woman derive inspiration or achieve grace from a book in which the only exemplary women are women deprived of their sexual nature?"

"Maybe I don't think everything revolves around sex," said Mercy. "What I

want is to attain what men have. Their intelligence. Their way of reasoning. I want to be strong in the way men are strong."

"What about the ways in which a woman can be strong?"

"They don't appeal to me. I think men are superior because they have a greater capacity for spirituality and rational thought. Women are too intuitive and earthbound."

"It sounds to me as if you have been taken prisoner by an idealised father," said Silvana.

"There's no need to idealise my father. He is perfect. Both my parents are perfect. I couldn't possibly ask for more loving parents."

"Are you sure you're not simply frightened of sexuality? Your attitude seems a little on the fanatical side to me. You know, don't you, that fanaticism is always an indication of suppressed fear and the desire to control it - usually fear of the unknown."

"I think anyone who isn't frightened of the unknown must be a fool. And anyway, I'm not sure the object of all fear is to find a cure for itself. God ought to instil fear."

In front of a reclining nude, Rowan was talking with one of Jared's students.

"I once told Jared that he was King Arthur and we were his knights of the Round Table," said Edward.

"What did he say?"

"He loved it. Whenever he gives me a critique he points to my paintbrush and says, Excalibur, Edward, Excalibur! He even mentioned it to my father. That was a mistake. My father is the voice of reason. You don't mention things like King Arthur to him. King Arthur? Realms of fantasy and poppycock. He thought Jared drank too much. I think he wanted to give Jared a stiff talking to. I shouldn't even be at the studio. It's sacrilegious according to my Christian group. It's blasphemous to make images of the things God created."

"We make images in our imagination all the time; I don't see it makes much difference if you put them down on canvas or sing yourself to sleep with them."

"But of course you would say that. You've never heard the Word." Edward let out a loud laugh full of mockery. "I've been hallucinating for two months now. Sometimes I see this figure that wears my clothes except let me tell you, he's jolly nasty. Not at all the kind of person you'd want to share your clothes with. I think Florence is a dangerous place. It's like being in the mind of a mad genius. There's too much weird energy here. Florence is making me mad."

"So what do you two boys think of the pictures?" asked Siobhan. There was an artificial red flower in her peroxide blonde hair and the line of her wet mouth was eloquent of erotic insinuation.

"Edward has just been telling me that it's blasphemous to make images. Only God is allowed to make images."

Edward laughed nervously. "God is love," he said.

"There I beg to differ," said Siobhan. "In the early books of the Bible God was an irritable partisan despot who more or less made things up as he went along. He had no concept of love until someone - was it Moses or Joseph? - showed him love."

Over in another corner of the room, near the table where the drinks were served, Andrew Hayward-Salt said, "Can I just say, Jared, that I think your Descent from the Cross is one of the most beautiful paintings I've ever seen."His earnestness, re-enforced by the stiff hauteur of his shoulders and his erect head, was so pronounced as to arouse a suspicion of subtle mockery.

"Well thank you very much, Andrew," said Jared, thrown into something of a quandary between embarrassment and flattered pride.

"I'm serious. Actually Jared, I wanted to talk to you about something. My uncle has an estate on the island of Cephalonia. I've told him about you and he's very keen on inviting a select few over this summer. They're carrying out an archaeological dig on his land at the moment so we would be able to participate a little in the excavations."

"That could be interesting. Algernon!" called out Jared, who in social gatherings was easily distracted. "I've had an idea. I want you to give a series of lectures on the Greeks. I know you prefer the Romans. Admit the truth, Algernon, you do go in for the Roman swagger style."

"To tell the truth, I can't say I've ever actively thought of myself in terms of swaggering."

"Too busy swigging to swagger? Do we actually ever see you in the mornings? The late-night drinking might just be getting a little out of hand. But to get back to what I was saying, as well as the philosophers, I want you to lecture on the *Iliad* and the *Odyssey* and then perhaps the *Oresteia* and the *Bacchae*."

"Lordy, we'll be dealing with some pretty ferocious women then. Clytemnestra was one angry vindictive wife."

"How about if I gave a lecture, Jared," said Siobhan.

"On what?"

"Moral aesthetics."

Jared smiled. "Are we though ready for Siobhan's moral aesthetics? Algernon? What do you think?"

"Siobhan is a frightfully bright girl."

"I don't doubt that. Here's Julian. Let's ask Julian what he thinks."

"About what, Jared?" asked Julian.

"About Siobhan and her desires."

"Who said anything about desire?" asked Siobhan, curling a lock of her hair around her little finger.

"Desire only burns in order to burn itself out, Jared," smiled Julian.

"You're so imperturbable, Julian. Is this your karma idea? That what happens happens and all we can do is to accept it?"

"Something like that, Jared."

"So I ought to let Siobhan give us a lecture on moral aesthetics? Algernon on poetics and Siobhan on aesthetics."

When everyone left the exhibition, Diane stood in front of the picture of herself as Leda being abducted by the swan. Diane was still uncertain as to why she had taken a lover. She had never been a promiscuous or gratuitous woman. Feeling unappreciated by her husband, she had gone through a phase of being susceptible to the flatteries of other men. It had all been harmless flirting. But Angelo d'Alba was persistent. To begin with, he represented not much more than a reproach or a warning to her husband. She imagined Jared a witness to the entire ritual and that he would become as a result chastened and attentively repentant. Everything she did she had done with Jared in mind. Nothing was really crystallised until she knew what Jared thought of it. He however remained headlocked in his own internal dramas. She had been deceiving him for months and months. Yesterday Angelo had left his wife and two children. Now he was pressuring her to leave Jared before the week was out.

14

Vivienne was on the phone to her father. His booming voice, so well adapted to public speaking, seemed to seek a larger audience. The clarity of his consonants and vowels was like the crisp unyielding leather of the armchairs in some exclusive men's club.

"We've just moved into our divine new flat," she told him. "We have a garden with two palm trees, a fig tree and rose bushes. It's enclosed on one side by the old city wall near San Niccolò."

"San Niccolò! How I love to hear the names of Florence's churches. Did you know that when the forces of Charles V were besieging *la città di Firenze*, Michelangelo hid in the belfry of *la chiesa di San Niccolò*? I'd love to return to Florence. Perhaps I shall come out in the autumn. How about it, old girl?"

"I'd love you to come out."

"Have you heard from your mother at all?"

"The last I heard she was helping out in some centre for the homeless. Why don't you give her a call?"

"She's such a saint but I'm not, I'm afraid to say, in her good books at present."

"Daddy, I don't suppose you remember a man called Sparks? I met a man here who says he knew you while you were in Florence. He's a barrister."

"One met so many people when one was in Florence and, to be perfectly honest, my memory is not what it was. Sparks, Sparks..."

"He's got demonic eyebrows and a kind of supernatural air of not inhabiting his body."

78

"Heavens above! Why do you ask?"

"No particular reason. I just wondered. He didn't seem to like you very much."

"Oh my goodness. As I remember, the men I knew in Florence were rather a touchy competitive crowd. It wasn't very difficult to get on the wrong side of them, especially if there was a woman involved."

"Was there a woman involved?"

"I really can't remember, my dear. I was speaking in generic terms. Anyway, I'm afraid I have to go now. Do send Siobhan my love. How is the old girl?"

"She's well. But you're sure you don't remember Damien Sparks?"

"What kind of barrister did you say he was?"

"He's a defence lawyer specialising in cases of fraud."

"Doesn't ring any bells."

"One last thing, I remember someone once telling me, it might have been Uncle Jack, that you were in love with a woman when you were here in the sixties."

"A woman? Uncle Jack said? I dare say there might have been a harmless crush. One does tend to be fanciful when one is a young man. To be honest I don't remember any specific woman."

"A married woman," said Vivienne detecting a nervous resilience in her father's tone.

"Good heavens! Uncle Jack has clearly got his wires crossed."

After the call Vivienne began trying things on in front of the mirror - a red dress, a pair of white jeans and a black jumper lay discarded around her bare feet.

"You're making quite a fuss over darling Rowan," said Siobhan. "I almost feel betrayed seeing as how he clearly disapproves of me."

"You like it when men disapprove of you."

"He obviously fancies you otherwise why would he invite you out for a drink?" said Nadia.

"Rowan's not clean enough for you," said Siobhan. "You

always go for that scrubbed look. The neat dry singed hair and well-pressed clothes. Boys who are slightly effeminate in their toilette and who will be bald by the time they're thirty. Like dreadful Andrew Hayward-Salt."

Vivienne laughed though she was also a little taken aback. "Do I?"

"By the way, Vivienne, I love your underwear! Molto sexy," said Nadia.

"Present from Siobhan. She's always spoiling me."

"Darling," said Siobhan, "why don't you wear my black mini skirt? The one I wore to ensnare Algie?"

"Did Siobhan tell you how she seduced Algernon?"

"Oh you don't want to hear about Algie. Though I must say he's certainly leaving his mark on me. Look at the bruises he inflicted on my thighs last night." Siobhan lifted up her skirt and pulled down her tights.

"Siobhan!" exclaimed Nadia. "What on earth do you two do in bed?"

"Who said anything about beds?"

The bar's neon sign spilled some of its chemical red sheen over the pavement. Vivienne was late for her appointment with Rowan. She was also slightly nervous and when she spoke, mocking the pseudo post-modernist décor of the bar, her voice came back to her as shrill and tuneless. The bar had bright playground blue walls and pretend chrome pipes. "As if there weren't already enough pipes in the world," said Vivienne.

They sat down at a metallic table outside near a small riverside park. Behind the flowering lime trees they could hear the polyphonic exertion of engines producing movement along the road which linked two bridges. No two engines were pitched on exactly the same key and the counterpoint of their tones was like an urban caricature of the swelling and subsiding rhythms of waves breaking on a shore. At the next table a couple had begun arguing.

"I wish I knew what they were talking about. I'm so ashamed of myself for having picked up so little Italian. You can speak it, can't you? What are they arguing about?"

"The usual things," said Rowan. "Neither of them is particularly eager to hear the other's point of view."

"Siobhan and I have been talking about relationships," she said. "Do you believe in love? As anything but a biological trick or an exercise in dramatising oneself to oneself, I mean. Siobhan doesn't. What do you think of Siobhan?"

Rowan narrowed his eyes as if contemplating a difficult chess move. "We don't really get on."

"Why is that, do you think?" said Vivienne after blowing out a funnel of smoke.

"I think it's got a lot to do with sexual vanity. We don't fancy each other and we're both slightly offended that we fail to find a response in the other."

"I worshipped the ground Siobhan walked on at Oxford and yet here, I don't know, I find her a little affected. She's my best friend and I'm not knocking her. I just wouldn't mind hearing what someone else has to say about her."

"I remember the first time I met her she was going on about Florence being like Euro-Disney. A fifteenth-century Renaissance theme park."

"That was probably just her way of trying to make herself feel at home."

"But Florence is a real place. It's easy to dismiss Florence as being a backwater but its idealism does make one think. It doesn't promiscuously cater to the pleasure principle the way London does. Florence is like a surrogate father. Just being here is like talking to a very intelligent man. London, on the other hand, is forever changing its mind according to the whims of fashion. Florence in some way is the kind of father I would have liked. Nowadays the average father is just a bumbling mumbling buffoon with no more authority than a traffic warden."

"The last thing Siobhan is looking for is a surrogate father."

"Siobhan though always has to reduce the authentic into artifice," said Rowan. "She prides herself on being wild, unbridled, off-hand as if nothing's really worth her attention unless it can immediately be caricatured and tossed off as anecdote. That means she's living without an affirmative language."

"Everything is theatre for Siobhan. I think it's her way of erasing personal history. Or not attributing too much meaning to anything. She doesn't dwell on things. She doesn't quite dwell in them either. I think that's what undoes us - some predisposition we have to dwell on what we can't do anything about. Isn't that why we've had enough of history? We all know by now we're going to go on making the same mistakes. History's kind of lost its raison d'être. It's no longer exemplary. It's become at best entertainment. At Oxford Siobhan was the queen of cool. She is clever. And she's read a phenomenal amount. I remember when she graduated she wore her gown with a black mini skirt. Doesn't she attract you at all?"

"No. But then I've always had a morbid terror of being turned into a laughing stock." Rowan slipped his ring off his finger and pressed it to his lips. "By the way, I heard your father was in Florence in the sixties. I don't suppose he's ever mentioned a woman called Ivana? She was a family friend who was also here in the sixties," he lied.

"Ivana?" Vivienne tried to remember if she had ever heard the name of the woman her father had supposedly been in love with and realised the name had always been withheld. "No. He's never mentioned anyone called Ivana."

"What about Damien Sparks?"

"What about him?"

"He was here in the sixties as well, wasn't he? I don't suppose he's mentioned an Ivana?"

"No. Anyway," she said, sitting back in her chair having long since finished her vodka and tonic, "I should be getting back. I have to draw Laocoön tomorrow morning."

15

A maelstrom of wayward energies had converged over the city; the cold and blustering May evening defied and collapsed chronology. What had happened to spring? Tonight's weather seemed psychological; there was anger in it. It was hard for Jared not to take it personally.

In his bewildered state he found himself noticing how many entrances and exits in Florence took the form of dark beckoning arches. His eye was drawn to the grotesque stone carvings ornamenting many of the old palaces - nightmare images, underworld threshold guardians, here a Cyclops, there a ferocious mutant with bat wings. Had they even existed yesterday? The city seemed to have unleashed ghouls as if to commemorate his own exile from the habitual world. He looked up to the dark smoking flames of the cypresses on the slopes for some respite but they too smouldered with intimations of loneliness and death.

When a bell tolled, the silence the echoing chimes left in their wake washed over the city like a departing wave. Jared followed the course of the Vasari Corridor, walking in the shadow of buildings where history was painstakingly preserved. History, its artistic patrimony rather than its crusades and revolutions, had always played a pivotal ordering role in his life. Masaccio had clearly come before Leonardo who in turn patently preceded Caravaggio - an evolution was discernible. He expected his personal life to follow a similar pattern. By betraying him Diane had rewritten history; his faith in its scriptures had been undone. If one act can alter the entire reading of a personal relationship might not the same be true of any history? What any more was sacred? Jared felt he was on the verge of a world stripped of all its transfiguring creeds.

Diane had told him about her betrayal at Pèlago. Resisting an urge to cast his wedding ring into the water, he had said to her, "Then I can no longer help you." Later they had laid down side by side on the grass together, like two frozen images on a Gothic funerary stone. A solitary yellow rose had opened its petals in the vicinity of the waterfall. "Why didn't you stop me?" she had asked in tears. "Why did you give me so much freedom? I tried to warn you, but you were oblivious."

He still loved his wife, still recognised her as part of his wholeness. Had his eyes been clouded by Mercy? I was distracted, he thought. I was blinded by Eve. I still can't get out of my mind the image of her with the black serpent eye. She was smouldering at me. Diane has gone forever. I don't want her back. That's what she's got to understand. I don't ever want to speak to her again. Now she has fallen, and I will no longer be there to listen. Let her face the consequences of her actions. She's broken up a family. She's betrayed me. She's betrayed her daughter by her first marriage and she's betrayed our daughter.

The faint river smell brought back nights when he and Diane had communicated in a simple language and fallen asleep in a tangle of tired limbs. How proud he had been of his elegant French wife. He remembered the glow of satisfaction the first time he had taken her to America to meet his mother and father. Through her he had crossed a threshold, had entered into a new phase of being - she led him irrevocably into the future. She was the woman who was going to make a man of him.

As he crossed Ponte Santa Trìnita and passed the statue of the shivering naked male on the far side, he remembered again the place where she had been betraying him. Only afterwards had he come across the word *pelago* amongst the opening lines of the *Inferno*. *Pelago - lo passo che non lasciò già mai persona viva.*

He saw himself stumbling blindly in the dark wood, through the voracious underbrush and the exposed tangled roots of prickly shrubs when Diane had led him down the stream. The croaking of the ubiquitous mating toads, seeping up from a deeper depth than any experience of the eye, had sounded like a summons from the pit of hell. Pèlago - the pass that never yet left anyone alive.

Jared entered the backroom of the studio and sat down in front of his large painting. His eye was drawn to the image of his wife. There she was beneath the fiery horizon line wearing the emerald stone around her neck. He stared hard at the face he had so beautifully painted. She now seemed to be bidding him to say farewell to her.

Her head was cradled by her daughter Francesca whose Italian boyfriend he had forbidden to attend Cordelia's first communion because they had entered into a carnal relationship. The old puritan had risen in him, the legacy of his father's education. His severity, his moral pretension now struck him as nothing short of ridiculous. On the day of Cordelia's communion, he now recalled, the relentless barking of his dog had led him to a dying baby bird. He had arrived in time to witness the weak pulse in its twisted neck beat out its final communion with life. The bird had closed its eyes on the world under his gaze. When he came to think what it might mean in personal terms he thought perhaps it simply signified the passing of Cordelia's childhood; now he realised the death of the baby bird had communicated a darker prophecy.

Jared noticed again the mistrustful way his daughter was looking at Magdalene. She in the picture was the divine child. Someone had once said that it was in the glint of Cordelia's eye that the resurrection was anticipated. A drop of Christ's blood fell on her, like a kind of dew. He had painted that drop of blood on Cordelia's head exactly where he had been hit while gathering up the crown of thorns for his Christ. Did that mean his daughter would suffer the effects of his own wound? In the painting the highlight in Cordelia's eye was just about the only glimmer of hope, if it was hope - after what Diane had done he saw only fear and sadness in his daughter's eye.

He walked forward to look more closely at the image of his wife and felt as though he had been betrayed by his own creation. He had snatched Diane away from her first husband. Was it not inevitable that there would be hell to pay for that? You cannot anger one of the gods without retribution. Once again it occurred to him that the Christ with one hand still nailed to the cross was an image of himself. He was leaning down towards his wife, his right arm outstretched towards her. He had begun his sacrificial descent.

The last day Jared, Diane and Cordelia spent as a family they visited a fair famous for its miniature reproductions of many of Europe's famous cities. Jared and Diane thus walked through shrunken copies of places they had visited together - Vienna, Paris, London. Finally, they arrived in the downscaled Florence, except only a small section of the city was represented, the area around Santa Croce where Diane and he had lived throughout their marriage. Diane began crying. Jared found himself holding her hand.

Cordelia, her eyes downcast, timidly persuaded her father to take her for a ride on the ferris wheel. Diane was frightened of heights and watched from below as they spun round and round in the garishly painted bucket. Looking down at her watching him and Cordelia, Jared, as the creaking wheel began another descent, remembered a line from the Bible that his father used to quote: *Man, if indeed thou knowest what thou doest, thou art blessed; but if thou knowest not, thou art cursed, and a transgressor of the law.* When the ferris wheel stopped he and his daughter were for a while suspended up high in mid-air.

16

The arrival of the fairies coincided with a phone call from Diane. Jared had passed the morning wandering into churches, gazing up at altars, contemplating side chapels, crucifixes, angels. Was he simply hoping to find some freedom in his thinking, or was he seeking retribution? The Christian way was to turn the other cheek. To forgive. But he was not prepared to forgive, not prepared to play into Diane's hands. She had committed an outrage, she had broken a sacred bond and he could not and did not want to find forgiveness within himself. He wished her to suffer. His thinking circled this one source of pain; there was no exit. She now tricked him into entering into a dialogue. Having taken away Cordelia, she now wanted the dog too.

"It's my dog, Jared."

"You know what Francesca thinks, don't you? She thinks you've gone mad."

"We need to talk."

"There's nothing to say. You've broken up a family, Diane."

"I understand that you're angry."

Jared slammed down the phone.

An hour later the fairies, as Jared was to call them, clambered out of an old dirty white van which pulled up outside the studio. The fairies were a group of travelling street performers including a former student. Jared gave them permission to camp out in the huge oval room. Rowan too was present to witness their arrival. The previous night he had spent the evening with Jared in his apartment. They had been alone in what struck him as a room echoing with absence. Jared had withdrawn into a corner of the room near his desk and sat with his back to the two large bookshelves which stood at the far end of a wide expanse of parquet floor. Diane had removed most of the furniture and with it all trace of any female presence. "It's returned to its original nature - a bachelor's pad," said Jared. "Perhaps that's my true nature too? Perhaps I was never really supposed to get married."

"I can't see myself getting married," said Rowan.

"Once upon a time the penalty for infidelity was death. We think of such measures now as barbaric but what about wantonly breaking up a family? Is that then to be condoned? We'd have no Greek tragedy, no Shakespeare if mankind had always sanctioned betrayal as a natural consequence of the marriage bond. Have we really evolved or are we simply now forced to repress our deeper feelings. Nowadays we're expected to remain friends. We're expected to make the peace with the man who has destroyed our family. We're supposed to forgive. That's the Christian point of view."

The alpine early evening blue of Jared's eyes had not tonight been so evident. No conduction of the heat of his anger had taken place. He continued to bring his fist down hard on any surface available. Rowan was sometimes at pains to defend himself from the haemorrhaging fury of Jared's mind. Not having found love Rowan was at a loss to know what losing it might feel like. Neither had he ever sat alone with anyone in such emotional pain. Jared, he knew, was trying to put his life back together. His present inability to extend the range of his emotions took him to the threshold of coherency. There were after all only so many ways you could say the same thing. What though was the alternative to anger? Sadness might lead to self-pity and emasculation. Jared had emerged from the betrayal wielding a sword.

He had continued to invoke the name of his wife's lover. "Who is the angel of the dawn? Lucifer is the morning star. Isn't that the same thing? I painted her as the Virgin Mother and she's betrayed me with Lucifer." When Rowan had ventured to suggest that it was counterproductive to dwell on his wife's culpability, that by insisting on this one line of thought he was simply re-living the same moment over and over again in his mind, Jared began shouting at him. "You're really rather naïve, Rowan, do you know that? You've never had a long-term relationship." Later, exhausting his anger, he became more philosophical. "It seems there will always be three stages in the life of the male. There is the Tristan stage - the falling in love, the love grotto removed from the everyday world; then there is King Arthur – the slings and arrows stage; and then there is the Anfortas stage - the sexual wound. The fourth element, the hidden fourth, to make up the quaternity would be Perceval - the redeemer."

In relation to Jared, Rowan was forced to acknowledge how chameleon-like was his own social persona. Never did he fight to impose his order, never did he take pains to assert a conflicting outlook. Did he then have no convictions of his own? Perhaps he spent most of his life harbouring an eagerness to return to his solitude because so often he was at the mercy of the personality of the person with whom he was engaged? To Rowan, the classifications to which Jared resorted to create an idea of order seemed often nothing but unseeded rhetoric, like shouting at a force of nature. However, there was power in the boundaries the older man created.

"We might be in *A Midsummer-Night's Dream*," said Rowan as they watched the troupe strew their tattered belongings over the oval room's brick floor and a boy with white dreadlocks dance in circles with a shaven-headed girl wearing a flouncy stained red ballgown from another era.

"Are they fairies or are they trolls?" asked Jared. "Perhaps the trolls have arrived. What's going on, Rowan? First my wife leaves me and then the trolls arrive. Is Damien behind it all? Mephistopheles would be accompanied by trolls, wouldn't he?"

Rowan smiled uncomprehendingly.

"That's Ewan," Jared continued, nodding towards the boy with thinning blonde hair who was talking to Mercy. "He used to be a student of mine. I like him even if he is a troll. There is something maimed about Ewan though. Is that the law of opposites? The macho façade disguising the emotional scars? I just noticed how ugly his hands are. They are not the hands of an artist. I have problems with my hands. I'm allergic to turpentine but they are the hands of an artist. Many women have said this. But he's dynamic in his quiet brooding way. Mercy already seems quite taken by him."

"She flirts with everyone."

"And Sir Daryl is one bitter and disillusioned knight. He's finally realised that *la belle dame sans merci* rubbing her leg against his isn't a coded erotic invitation but merely what she resorts to in order to get attention. He's given me an ultimatum - either she goes or he does."

"Apparently she's had enough of Florence and is about to leave," said Rowan.

"Let her go. It's time Mercy went. Do we all have to bow down to her moods the whole time? I'm not entirely sorry she's going. She was though the perfect Eve."

The street performers, chatting excitedly in a variety of languages, were changing into their costumes. They were dressing up as eight of the characters in the tarot.

"Who are you supposed to be?" asked Jared of Ewan and the girl by his side. They both had several small hearts poorly painted in lipstick on their faces.

"We're the lovers, but don't ask me why. It was Narcisse's idea. He's the guy with the white dreadlocks. He won't wear anything that isn't white or eat anything that isn't white. We're only along for the ride."

"And this is your girlfriend?"

"No. This is Tara. She's seeing a French chef, aren't you?"

The girl smiled.

"Diane and I had our tarot cards read once," said Jared,

momentarily closing his eyes. "It was her idea. I got the Hanged Man, who is a kind of inverted Christ figure. I was told I would soon start on a big project as a result of an accident and that though this would be successful there would also be some darkness in my life. Diane got the Tower. An image of chaos and destruction. Two figures tumbling to ground beneath a bolt of lightning. There's also a falling crown."

Narcisse in his white robes now stood beside Tara.

"You look like the Priest," Jared told him. "Is there a Priest in the tarot? I know there's a Priestess."

"I'm the Magician."

"Then you have to adopt the Magician's stance," said Jared. "One arm stretched up, the other pointing down. As above, so below."

Narcisse immediately assumed the pose and, bewitchingly, held it for more than a minute.

The troupe executed their performance in front of the Baptistery that evening. The eight characters, attracting a sizable crowd of tourists, shuffled around without apparent rhyme or reason. Jared repeatedly asked Rowan what it all meant.

"It must mean something. It's not every day a troupe of nomad minstrels turns up dressed as tarot card figures."

Jared's eye was attracted to the two pretty girls. Both dressed in an outlandish caricature of feminine docility, they moved around like dolls on invisible wires. They looked sedated. It occurred to Jared that he had married a sedated woman. Diane had been taking tranquillisers throughout their marriage. Did this mean he had never truly yielded up to a woman in full possession of her powers?

To his left, a few yards away, Mercy was also watching the performance. Jared could feel defensive anger stirring in him every time his eyes met those of Mercy whose doleful expression was, he knew, a reproach levelled at him personally. Hadn't she too betrayed him? Left him with a half-finished painting that he would never now be able to finish? At the final count he was hurt by her lack of gratitude, disappointed in her failure to have grown at the studio. No one was not expendable - he wanted her to know this. He would not be held to ransom by the selfish demands of one student. He was glad she was leaving.

Jared turned his attention to the Gates of Paradise. Adam and Eve expelled from Eden shimmering faintly with golden highlights. Not for the first time it struck him as odd that Diane's betrayal had coincided with the arrival of Eve. Once again, he could not help looking at Mercy and frowning. He then looked up at the sky which itself was a kind of aftermath, a battlefield of voids and burning dust. At the end of the performance she approached Jared and rather stiffly held out her hand.

"You're so spoilt, do you know that, Mercy?" he said, offended by the exhibitionism of her gesture. The girl burst into inconsolable tears. She had succeeded in casting him as the villain of the piece.

III

Sum Sine Regno

17

Flanked by hills from which white rocks jutted, the large mound of stony land bore a series of fresh wounds gouged into the earth with surgical precision. A series of eight adjacent trenches had been mapped out descending in a line from the highest point of the mound down its eastern slope. The pervasive stillness of the valley only accentuated the idea that something was waiting to be discovered. The wheelbarrows heavy with sifted soil were now pushed along the wooden planks with less frequency as the work became more intricate and exacting. Professor Notman, head of the expedition, was convinced the island known now as Cephalonia was actually the mythical Ithaca - as indeed the locals called it - and hoped, beneath this mound, to find the last of the great Homeric Bronze Age cities: Ulysses' home.

Jared and several of his students were staying in a house on the other side of the valley. The first time they visited the dig, Milena was down on her knees in a trench scraping the deposit off a fragment of what was guessed to be an arched portal.

"Found anything interesting?" asked Julian, looking down at her. He stood with his arms folded over the bib of his brown dungarees.

"Everything of any interest seems to be found in everyone else's trench so far," said Milena. Her smile was both brimming with chaste hoarded treasure - eloquent of how expensively she tended herself - and tethered by a reflex of self-deprecation.

"The further down you dig though the richer the bounty I would imagine," said Julian.

Milena climbed out of the deep gash in the ground to greet her new acquaintances. On the edge of another trench Professor Notman was talking to Andrew Hayward-Salt, Vivienne and Costanza.

"But isn't this amazing, Julian?" said Jared, back on Greek soil for the first time since his bachelor days. "Do you realise we might actually be standing on the spot where Ulysses defeated the suitors? I can't believe you've never read Homer, Julian. Really you ought to be ashamed of yourself. In the *Odyssey* you'll find this idea of the stringing of the bow, an idea that has always fascinated me. To string the bow is perhaps the idea of male action - the moral will. Sometimes one has to rise up and act. You won't know this having never read the book but Ulysses' son is a kind of Hamlet figure – he's indecisive, at least to begin with, until he's reproached, I forget by whom, maybe Menelaos. He's failing in his role as the heir apparent. The palace is overrun by parasites and reprobates, the queen is being courted by a succession of suitors. Nothing but disrespect is being shown the king in his absence. Isn't that a striking metaphor for the present state of things? Look at my own wife, for godsakes."

Julian folded his arms and looked dutifully around, including a backward glance over his shoulder. "So this is where they believe Ulysses' palace to be buried?"

"Yes! And we're a part of it! I thought those days were over with Evans, Schliemann and Blegen but just look around. I actually met Blegen while studying in Athens in the sixties. He gave a lecture. The machinery might be more sophisticated but otherwise we're witnessing a spectacle which belongs to the great halcyon days of archaeology."

At dinner Jared was at the head of the table. His outward celebration of the moment seemed to know no responsibility save that of assigning consequence to the evening over which he presided. The conversation began with Professor Notman explaining his reasons for choosing Cephalonia rather than Ithaca as the site for his excavations. The talk then turned to

Ulysses. Jared asked the archaeologist what he made of the *Odyssey*.

"Well, the *Iliad* is maybe the most macho book ever written. All that bronze on bronze brutality of men pitting their strength against each other. The *Odyssey*, on the other hand, is much more subtle. I think of it as a poetic rendering of a man's struggles to reconcile himself to the female. It's man coming to terms with his anima in all its guises. It's a far more sophisticated book than the *Iliad*. Really quite remarkable for its time."

"It is remarkable," said Jared, excited. "But what do you make of this idea of stringing the bow? You string the bow and take aim. Could it mean attaining mastery of one's craft? The act of creation?"

"Shooting an arrow is often an act of destruction," said Vivienne who despite summer had retained her pale complexion.

"What about Cupid's arrows? Love is an act of creation. Or are you one of these people, Vivienne, who no longer believes in love, just pleasure?" said Jared.

"Love surely is pleasure," she said leaning forward with a teasing smile.

"In its early stages certainly. But," said Jared turning back to the archaeologist, "what do you think, Josh? You don't mind me calling you Josh, Josh?"

"Not at all, Jared."

"Of course, stringing the bow and taking aim might also be construed as sexual. Could it be a sexual metaphor? Ulysses is after all about to reclaim his wife."

"One does have a soft spot for Penelope," said Professor Notman, uncertainly.

"Despite her deceptions? Her faith does after all begin to waver. She's beginning to entertain ideas. Do women always entertain ideas? Of course, men certainly do."

"Eighteen years is a long time," ventured Professor Notman.

"It is a long time. I was married for eighteen years but my Penelope ran off with a suitor. Have you had your Penelope, Josh?"

Professor Notman made the faintest nod of his head.

"But what about the idea of the night sea journey and the homecoming? Was it a spiritual journey, do you think? Does Ulysses really have his revelation? You see, I've just embarked on my own night sea journey. Not by choice - but then how much of what we do do we actually choose? Have you read the wonderful Tennyson poem about Ulysses? The implication is that there's a kind of second journey after Ulysses has won back his kingdom. How does the last line go? *To strive, to seek, to find, and not to yield.* How about a toast? I propose we drink a toast to the stringing of the bow."

Everyone clinked glasses. Milena, in her thin lilac dress, Jared noticed, looked radiant in the light of the candles.

"So tell me, Josh," said Jared, "how's Milena doing?"

"She's doing very well."

Milena lowered her eyes and a shy smile broke over her wide mouth. When she looked up, she avoided eye contact with the two men opposite and instead found her attention seized by a star visible through the open window.

"I hope you're going to visit us in Florence," said Jared. "We're opening up a sculpture studio soon. How about sculpture? Does the idea appeal to you or not?"

"I've always wanted to sculpt," said Milena.

"There you go. We need talented people, don't we, Julian?"

Later that night Milena walked away from the lights of the house towards the sea. Cicadas chanted in the tall grass and the fireflies perforated the deep darkness with their elusive watery lights. Branches which struck her as being sentient began to catch at her clothes as though making some urgent demand. Glimmers of mother-of-pearl appearing and disappearing in the near distance that she could trace back to no source disorientated her.

When the view broadened and she had before her the great black sweep of the sea, she clambered down a rocky slope and sat against the trunk of a pine tree. She could smell the salt of the sea behind the earthy fragrance of the pine resin and licked her wrist, enjoying the taste of brine on her skin. The high moon resembled her childhood moons when she had felt the future coiled up inside her like a sleeping serpent. Out of the corner of her eye she was aware now and again of the changing forms of the waves and flashes of suddenly heightened light. She could hear the tide sucking at the fossilised rocks beneath her, swirling in and out of hidden crevices and secret underground channels.

18

Katherine Cripwell sat at the large kitchen table dabbing antiseptic onto the small cut on her finger. "Now let me get this straight," she said, glancing briefly in her daughter's direction. "You've been to a Greek island to dig up lots of old bones?"

"Every old bone has a story to tell," said Milena. She was prepared for her mother's tone, at once pragmatic and disparaging.

"But you don't know the first thing about archaeology."

"I was simply a volunteer, one of the people that help sift through the soil," said Milena, resting the mug of tea she cupped in both hands against her bottom lip.

"What use is a skinny girl like you with a shovel? You always used to shy away from any form of physical activity. We never could get you to ride a horse or even play tennis."

"I wasn't digging. They have machines for that. I was simply down on my knees in a trench with a trowel or a spatula."

"But there are skeletons buried in the earth. Just thinking about it gives me the creeps. I don't understand why people want to rake up the past. Why can't people just let sleeping dogs lie?"

"Then we'd know far less about our history," said Milena, as a matter of course.

"And what has history ever taught us? Like nature, it only goes on repeating itself. Knowing about something doesn't stop it from happening again."

"I've also decided to go to Florence for a while. The dig doesn't begin again until April so I thought I'd do a sculpture course there."

"What's brought all this on?"

"All what on?"

"I don't know. All this restlessness."

"I like travelling and I feel like I'm stuck in a rut in London. I'm just drifting aimlessly."

"And what about Tom, what does he think about you leaving the country?"

"We've split up."

"I thought you two got on well. He seemed like a nice young man."

"You didn't like him when I was going out with him."

"I was put off by his appearance. He looked like one of those animal rights protesters with his dreadlocks and his scruffy clothes. We had a nice chat about the orchard when he came down that Sunday. He gave me lots of good advice about the garden. I saw then that he took his landscape gardening seriously. Before that, I thought he was just a layabout. That, after all, is the impression he seems to want to give."

Mrs. Cripwell walked over to where the clock her mother had given her ticked loudly on a shelf and said,

"I've told you, haven't I, that I went to Florence as a young woman. I spent a month there."

"Doing what?"

"Oh, just idling my time away. I was at a low ebb and friends offered me their flat for a month, so I just went."

"Without Dad?"

"He was working."

"What year was this?"

"Oh, I can't remember. Sometime in the sixties."

Katherine lay in her arctic double bed unable to concentrate on the book she was reading. Milena had always aroused in her complex emotions and was often on her conscience. This, no doubt, was due to the circumstances of her birth. Was it wrong of her to have never told Milena the truth? She sensed tonight there was something Milena had not told her. Had she perhaps begun to suspect the truth? What was the truth? She herself wasn't entirely sure how to make a narrative of what had happened in Florence. Getting out of bed and going over to her dressing table she realised Milena's talk of excavations and Florence had, if not woken, then disturbed in their slumber several sleeping dogs.

She could not guess at the enthusiasms and ambitions Milena did not share, the exasperations and defeats to which she gave no voice. Every maternal impetus burnt itself out on the passivity of her daughter's reflexive smile. Milena, she sensed, gave the barest minimum to preserve intact her emotional alliances. To ask for more was to receive less. She would not suffer her soil to be raw and tender, would not submit to the vulnerability of the new green shoot. Katherine wondered if this was her fault. No one though could accuse Milena of being contentious. She had a ready smile, shunned argument and her rebellions had all been aesthetic - a fondness for exotic jewellery, colouring her hair and floating around in long bright coloured gypsy skirts.

Katherine returned to her bed with an envelope of photos from her stay in Florence. The first evidence she sought was the extent of her aging process. How much had she changed to look at? There she was in an alarmingly short skirt in front of the church of Santo Spirito. The flaking plaster of the eastern wall gave little indication of the exalted harmonies of the church's interior and she could not help comparing the disparity between exterior and interior to her own situation. Her face, when it jumped unexpectedly out of mirrors at her, as it did now, often struck her as a contradiction of everything she felt to be true about herself. She saw shadows and harsh lines which seemed to indicate that her true self, still stocked with virginal candles yet to be lit, had sunk beneath a hardening enamel.

19

Milena was holding a bunch of wildflowers she had picked herself in the country lanes behind San Miniato. During her walk down the hill the flowers and the attention they attracted from passers-by made her self-conscious. She began to experience them as an offering or emblem of her vulnerability. She gazed down at their variety of tubular corollas, sticky pistils, creamy stamens and offerings of pollen. To be made to feel as gracefully beautiful as the precocious spike of these wine-red petals twisting on their erect ballerina stalks was surely a natural imperative in the secret heart of every woman.

She had been in Florence for two weeks. In the mornings, having cycled to the school along the river, she was part of a small group sculpting the figure model in the studio downstairs at the back of the building. Kneading form and rhythm out of the earthy clay was a source of pleasure fraught with frustration. What though is happiness if not the overcoming of obstacles? Every breakthrough she made rippled a secret replenishing pleasure through her body. In the afternoon she joined the class engaged in a charcoal figure drawing when her eye and hand were called upon to reproduce the soft shadows made by the tendons, veins and muscles beneath the surface of flesh.

The gravel path in the large garden was marked at intervals by a weathered statue of a nymph or goddess. In the sky the colours of the sunset still lingered. The darkening expanse of the palazzo evoked the mystery of its long history. Milena had come here with Vivienne for a dinner party Julian and Costanza were hosting. A man in a black sheepskin coat had been waiting by the gate when they entered the grounds of the palace. Milena now followed behind him and Vivienne. She felt uncomfortable because she could hear everything they said.

"I asked Dad if he knew you and he said he'd never once heard of you." There was the hint of a shrill note in Vivienne's voice.

"Perhaps PJ simply doesn't want to remember. He was, after all, pursuing a married woman at the time."

"Was her name Ivana? Rowan asked me about her."

"Rowan?"

"I'm pleased something is capable of surprising you. I was beginning to think you might be omniscient."

"I've always been good at gathering information. It is, after all, part of my job."

Dinner was served on a long candlelit wooden table in a secluded alcove of the garden. Milena was seated between Julian and Algernon. Opposite, the man who had accosted Vivienne at the gate was talking to Jared. He was telling a story about a mother weeping for her missing son which related to the plaque outside the studio. She got it into her head he was called Raphael, but later Algernon told her his name was Damien. Every so often she caught him looking at her. She felt he might be mistaking her for someone else and that she might be called upon to clear up some misapprehension.

Later, when Julian went off to make the coffee and the soothsaying stars were bright in the dark sky, Rowan sat down next to Milena.

"Like me, you're an only child. No brothers or sisters. That could be a bond between us," he said playfully. He picked up her bag from the ground and held it in his lap. "Is this a diary?" he said, running his finger over the red leather of a book inside the bag.

"It's a kind of diary."

"Can I read it?"

"No." She smiled. Rowan watched her moisten her upper lip with the tip of her tongue.

"Why?"

"It would make me feel very vulnerable."

"To feel vulnerable is often to feel more alive," he said, caressing a silver coin he took from his pocket. "I've noticed tonight that you play hide and seek with yourself."

Milena smiled and for the first time looked searchingly into his eyes. "What makes you think that?"

"The way you go in and out of focus. The way you pretend even to yourself that there's less to you than there really is."

Bowing her head and plucking at a fold in her fuchsia skirt, she smiled.

"You like to give the impression of being as malleable as wet clay, but I get the feeling there's a lot of guardian marble in you."

"Now you're speaking in riddles."

"It's how I keep life at bay. I like your ring," he said, reaching out his left hand to touch her left hand on whose little finger she wore a serpent ring.

"The three golds," she said, lowering her eyes so he saw their purple-smudged lids.

"Why have you come to Florence, do you think? The myth of the Latin Lover? A more civilised way of life? A nostalgia for the days when the father still imparted some exemplary fabric of spiritual integrity. Or simply to learn the salty swelling and subsiding rhythms of a Mediterranean language?"

"I'm hopeless at learning new languages," she said with a self-deprecation which even when not voiced was never not quite absent in the gainsaying gestures of her body.

When Rowan was called to the other end of the table by Jared, Damien Sparks sat himself down on the vacated chair and looked closely into Milena's mermaid blue eyes.

"I hear from Jared that your name is Cripwell. You're not by any chance Katherine's daughter?" he said. "All evening I've been baffled as to who you remind me of. I actually knew your mother when she was in Florence in the sixties. She was greatly admired during her stay here. I can think of at least three men who were in love with her. I don't suppose you've ever heard her mention someone called Max Ashworth? I often wonder what happened to him."

Milena shook her head.

"Jared tells me you've just participated in an archaeological dig in Greece. How was it digging up the past? Enjoyable? Or a little eerie?" he said, striking a match.

20

"And here's you as Circe turning men into swine," said Jared, having again turned the page of the illustrated book. "You're not going to do that at my studio, are you?"

Tara smiled radiantly, though her eyes disclosed little comprehension. Might she not smile radiantly whatever he said? Jared turned another page of the book – men on a reeling boat passing through an ambush of jutting chthonic rock. This was an illustration for children of the *Odyssey*. There was little text; the story was told in pictures. On the floor at Jared's feet lay a parallel version of the *Iliad*. Thus had Jared beheld a succession of images in which the female standing before him featured, often with one or both breasts exposed, in a hegemony of female roles: Helen, Calypso, Thetis, Circe and finally, his favourite image, Nausicaa.

After touring Europe with the troupe of street performers Tara had returned to Florence and now she was at a loose end and in need of money. Her large brown eyes in conjunction with her quick smile and flushed cheeks summoned an idea of body-warm generosity. Jared had detected a secret hurt in the girl and was intrigued. He had an unfinished Eve painting on his hands; this girl who had already posed as a whole host of female archetypes was offering herself as a model. He turned the page. There she was again, this time as Penelope, unravelling her loom. The idea of the faithful wife tautened a thread inside him but this faint stir of anger expired when he looked up and caught the candour in the uplifted line of her unpainted parted lips.

"The Island of the Sun," he said. "That's an interesting idea. There's the night sea journey and the island of the sun - the light and the shadow. What about you, Tara? Do you have a shadow side?"

"I try and go with the flow," she said.

"Wasn't she involved with a French chef," asked Jared, standing in the midst of a proliferation of dust down in the room below his personal studio.

Ewan nodded but without prising himself from his present task - the wrenching out of a rusted nail from a workbench. He was stripped down to a torn old t-shirt bleached of its original colours.

"How old is she exactly?"

"She's twenty-six."

"The same age as you," said Jared. "She showed me the reproductions of herself posing for those illustrated books of the *Iliad* and the *Odyssey*. Have you seen them? Don't you find that amazing? I have to use her as a model. I was waiting for a new Eve and a new Eve arrives. Somehow it's been decreed. She's got a great body - almost perfect. Perhaps her hands are a little coarse. You see, Ewan, I'm an aesthete," smiled Jared who could not help again noticing how ugly Ewan's hands were. "I like long tapering fingers in a woman. My wife had beautiful hands. But you know what Mercy said? She said one day, Jared, you'll find someone with more beautiful breasts than mine and paint over me. And do you know what? Her prophecy is going to come true. That's exactly what I'm going to do."

"Why don't you start a new picture?"

"You haven't seen my Mercy picture, have you? There are a lot of good things in it. It would be a waste to leave it unfinished. I'm not the prolific professional artist. It's not my nature to just bat out pictures. Every picture I do costs me a vast amount of my lifeblood. Not that I want to appear precious. It's simply the way I'm made. Of course, you know Leonardo didn't paint much. Maybe it's a question of temperament. Anyway, I think what you're doing is great. I've always wanted to offer a sculpture class."

"I thought we might do a figure project using Tara."

"That's a great idea. You can have her in the mornings, I'll have her in the afternoons."

Every day Jared awoke to the harrowing revelation that Diane had gone forever. The smell of Diane's scent still lingered in the apartment, recalling moments when she had answered his deepest needs. So pervasively sharp was the fragrance at times that the implication was she would soon be returning home. It was the task of his rational faculties to assure himself this was not the case. If there was a healing balm in his life it was not so much time as his new model. Tara was earthbound. She unfurled herself on sparkling sunlit waves of enthusiasm. She seemed to promise replenishment. He was often so physically close to her nakedness, so sequestered within its intimacy, that he felt he was able to register every nuance of her feeling on his own skin. Every day she brought with her a brown bag of fresh fruit which she shared with him during breaks. Time spent with this generous unspoiled girl was taking his mind off Diane and what she had done to him.

While light dwindled from the north-facing room and Tara stood thigh-deep in rising shadow Jared was to be found late every afternoon painting his Eve. He thrust forward his brush on a fully extended arm like a fencer and strode up to the canvas. Now, he thought, has arrived a Praxiteles Eve. She is not sloe-eyed like Mercy, her eyes are wide open in trust and her lips are parted in anticipation of sensual pleasure. Her naked shoulders, her naked belly, her perfect breasts are now my inspiration and perhaps even my desire. Eve, remember, fell for the wonder of love, yielded to her desire to know, to touch, to feel and as a result made known humankind.

"Who is that sculpture of up there in the niche?" asked Tara during a break.

"That's Venus," he said, studying his work in progress. He was superimposing his new Eve over the old image of Mercy. This though was proving difficult. Mercy would not relinquish her territorial rights. Tara had a different way of pivoting herself on her hips which created a problem of design he was at a loss to quite resolve.

He was out shopping for pigments and balsam Saturday afternoon when he met Tara by chance outside the church of Santa Felicita. On a whim he invited her inside to look at Pontormo's *Deposition*.

"I can picture your big painting in here," she told him. "It'd look amazing."

"Thank you," he said, startled into acknowledging how much shyness there still was in his nature. "It's a shame churches no longer commission works of art, which is perhaps one reason for the demise of the church and by the same token the demise of art." He walked with her across the aisle to a painting of an angel and an old man with a dog curled up asleep in the bottom right corner.

"I'd forgotten about this painting. This is Tobias restoring sight to his blind father," he said, struggling to peer through the oily sheen of reflected light on the canvas. "Have you ever looked at the plaque outside the studio? It's a bas-relief of Tobias with the Archangel Raphael. Damien was telling me the full story the other night. Raphael disguises himself as a mortal man – he's a kind of trickster – and accompanies Tobias on his quest to find his inheritance. Tobias' home, you see, has become an unhappy place. His father has been blinded, his mother is distraught. Tobias on his wanderings has to do battle with a leviathan fish in order to secure the healing balm not only for his father but also his future wife. She has been possessed by some demon."

"Or was that," said Tara, "simply what men liked to believe in those days whenever a woman spoke her mind?" When she turned to look at him there was an affectionate radiant smile in her eyes which Jared couldn't help not mirroring.

21

Out of the blue came the commission from a church in Alabama. Jared was asked to supply five large canvases celebrating the Holy Virgin to fill the apse of the Church of the Immaculate Conception. Negotiations were now underway with the American heiress whose job it was to convince the bishop.

Debates, held more or less every day, over how these pictures might be tackled offered much food for thought. The five paintings were to be the Angel of the Lord Appearing to the Shepherds, the Nativity, the Crucifixion, the Immaculate Conception and the Archangel Michael Vanquishing Satan. Prints of the great masters, especially Titian's *Assumption*, were pored over, questions of composition studied and argued over in detail, logistics surveyed and resolved; Jared, having re-read the apocalyptic *Revelations* for the first time since his university days, was in his element. His relationship to both art history and the Bible received a new animating impetus.

"I want to paint the Crucifixion and the Immaculate Conception myself. I already have an idea for the Crucifixion. As opposed to the deposed Christ – that's what my Descent is, the deposing of the king - and the Madonna unconscious on the ground, how about a Christ upright on the cross looking down at the mother, she too upright - the male and female communicating in strength instead of in defeat? How's that for an idea?"

"I think that's wonderful," said Costanza.

"And what about the actual Immaculate? I envision Mary standing upright, not seated, and a dove will act as a crown of thorns above. She'll be standing on the moon. In fact, what were we playing today? The beautiful *Virgin Mary Vespers* of 1610 by Monteverdi and in that there's the allusion to her standing on the moon. You're always pointing out, Julian, that in Velázquez the dove radiates light through the crown. I want to combine the Titian *Assumption* with the Velázquez *Coronation*. What elements would you like to see in the picture? Remember there are the saints on earth and the spirits in the sky."

"Why not make it a celebration of the female? Lots of angels escorting her up."

"Is this your idea that the great pagan Earth Mother is returning to claim her due in the form of the Madonna? Catholicism has kept alive the archetype. It's now her will that the West receives her?"

"People are tired of worshipping a male tyrant god, Jared. I remember at the community when one day, very mysteriously, a beautiful black marble sculpture of Kali arrived. Guru had a chapel built for it and that event marked a change in the spiritual identity of the community. Lots of people came because they were eager to worship a female deity. That, after all, is how our culture began."

"We can't though regress," said Jared, frowning.

"What we have once known we shall know again, in an altered form," said Julian with his jaunty habitual optimism.

"Let's not forget my studio is housed in a church. Is this the church reclaiming its true spirit? How's that for a synchronism? And not only is the church as a church demanding the continuance of its heritage so too is the church as atelier. What could be more appropriate? Is it possible this building itself has an evolutionary imperative? To paint religious pictures in a building which was created for religious purposes - isn't that a culmination of sorts? Evidence of an appointed end fulfilling itself?"

While negotiations were still underway, Julian and Costanza began painting a study of angels. Wings were required. It was suggested that they purchase a bird from a taxidermist. Julian objected. It was not right to paint into a religious painting the wings of a bird which had been callously shot. They tried to paint the wings from imagination. Then, one morning, Costanza and Julian were amazed to come across a dying pigeon by the studio door. Costanza, cradling it in the crook of her arm, took it upstairs and tried to nurse it back to health. Within two hours the bird had died. Julian and Costanza drove to Prato with it where a taxidermist severed and preserved its wings. There was a spiritual translucence in the appearance of the dying bird at that precise moment in time. Julian saw it as a sign of a deistic collusion. They were being aided and abetted in their task from on high.

Jared himself began a study of the Madonna, using Tara as his model. He laid down the first stroke, creating the angle of the brow to nose which at the studio was known as the Van Dyck Z. For the next half an hour he worked quickly, intensely. While working he thought about the mysterious act of applying paint to canvas. What guided the hand? When a fresh stroke of pigment was transferred from brush to canvas was it a purely physical act masterminded by the eye? Was it the channelling of a mental act through manual dexterity? Was it the confluence of a willed act acted upon by a kind of inspired undertow of the spirit or did an entire synthesis of forces flow down into the hand? Was it an act of love, like caressing and eliciting the desired response from the flesh of the lover? This painting of Tara in all probability would outlast her mortal life. She would become as he saw her.

"It's a strange twist of fate that some of the best heads ever painted in the history of art - Van Dyck's portraits of Charles I - were of someone who was to lose his head. Can you imagine that beautiful head being severed by an axe?"

Tara, who had never heard of Van Dyck until two weeks ago, shook her head. Before, while he had painted her as Eve, she had stood in her nakedness without self-consciousness; now dressed in blue robes she appeared less sure of herself.

"Often," he said to her, mixing colours on his palette, "the

Madonna is depicted standing on a globe and a serpent. In Titian's altarpiece, it's clouds. You really must go and see that painting. Have you never seen it?" He thought about inviting her to Venice for a weekend, was almost on the verge of doing so but the fear of a rejection held him back. Again he was forced to own up to his age in years. He was after all old enough to be her father. The next brushstroke he applied to his canvas was delivered by a hand sensitised by a shroud of sadness. To transpose a feeling into an act is to risk polluting the current which brought the feeling into being. Jared had invested in his new model the authority to administer or withhold a healing balm. Let her be idea and let idea suffice, he thought.

22

Katherine Cripwell walked past a succession of artisan work-shops smelling of varnishes and solvents. She was on her way to meet her daughter. It struck her as odd how little history she was able to call on to support her progress along streets which should have been poignantly familiar to her eye no less than to her senses. What she realised on returning to Florence was that she had been something of a sleeping beauty while here. So absorbed had she been in her own inner sonorities that she had collided with life rather than experience it as a synthesis or a reciprocal saturation.

When she turned the corner into Borgo San Frediano, it became more of an effort not to remember. Suddenly shocking it was to be forced into acknowledging how much time had gone by, how much of her life she had already heedlessly consumed. It sometimes seemed to her that life was like the unravelling of a relentless succession of knots in a thread that never revealed either its source or its destination. What did it all amount to? Does experience accumulate or does it simply melt into isolated iridescent puddles which gleam meaninglessly on an ever-thickening dark background? No story in which she had had a part had ever been satisfactorily resolved, no thread had ever been taken up where it was left off and yet one was encouraged to believe that every act or even desire in one's life was precipitated by the events that preceded it. Her spirit always retreated into a guarded seclusion of its own that she could track back to childhood.

The late autumn light was thin and without texture. Katherine walked as though she had drawn a mantle of invisibility around her. As she approached the studio she initially thought the man in the doorway must be a figment of her imagination.

"How extraordinary," he said with exactly the facial expression, as if he had just proved a point, which whenever she reluctantly remembered him he was apt to assume. "Extraordinary anyway if you are who I think you are."

"Hello, Damien," she said. She was barely aware of Damien Sparks introducing her to Jared Regis who, in turn, spoke to her of Milena and how well she was doing at the studio. A succession of scooters sped by close to the kerb, vomiting out black exhaust.

"Of course, you know, Jared, that it will soon be the anniversary of the flood. November 4th. As I recollect though, Katherine, you had already left Florence by then?"

"I left during the summer."

"An acquaintance of ours died in the flood. What was her name? The woman married to Max Ashworth."

"Ivana," said Katherine. She folded her arms over her breast and noticed for the first time a faint stain on her white cashmere sweater.

"Ivana. Of course. It was even said, I seem to remember, that she committed suicide. Apparently Max, her husband, was behaving atrociously. I wonder whatever happened to him. I don't suppose you've heard anything?"

"So have you never left Florence?" she said sharply to Damien.

"Oh I come and go." His eyebrows arched and contracted almost in the same moment.

"Milena's in the sculpture room. Why don't I lead you to her?" asked Jared. Through the large wooden door Katherine followed Jared and Damien into a high, darkened room where charcoal dust thickened the air and students were at work at their easels. They then passed through another wooden door and stepped into a vast storeroom. Hordes of sculptures all revealing wounds, cracks and missing limbs converged down on Katherine from all sides - a towering Christ on the cross hung beside a massive horse mounted by a male warrior while countless female deities and nymphs stood on shelves dulled by the dust of decades. The room was a cluttered narrative of aspiration. Out of the corner of her eye, behind a slumbering river god, she saw the low wooden door in the wall which led to the underground crypt where she had lost the sanctity of her naked self.

Jared pushed open another wooden door and they entered the sculpture room where Tara was posing for Ewan Slater and his class of students, one of whom was Milena.

At dinner, to which Jared but not Damien had been invited, Rowan was sitting opposite Milena's mother. Every time their eyes met over the table he perceived or imagined mistrust in her towards him. When she had asked him what his surname was he had felt she was dismissing him on social grounds as any kind of romantic candidate for her daughter.

"So you're not studying at the college?" she said. "You just happen to be in Florence."

"Rowan has posed for some fine paintings," interposed Jared. "In fact, I'd like to paint him one day. Don't you find there are certain physical similarities between him and Milena? Look at their noses and their brows."

Katherine drew her hand over her forehead as if to erase some perceived blemish there.

"So, Katherine," continued Jared, "you knew Damien when you were here in the sixties? How well did you know him?"

"Not very well. He was one of many English people in Florence at the time."

"Strange that you should meet up again though. Guido Locatelli, my landlord, told me about the parties held at the studio in the sixties. They sounded quite wild."

"I don't recall them as being any different from any other parties."

"Did you ever meet Guido? Unlike all his ancestors he doesn't sculpt. Milena is actually very talented. She has a very sensitive and natural feel for clay. Where does she get her talent from? You or her father?"

"Certainly not from me." She dabbed her mouth with a napkin. "So the big painting I saw is what you're presently working on?"

"The Descent from the Cross. Some people say it's too dark. But shadows are the mercurial element of a painting – it's they that create the transitions. Shadows not only have a life of their own but also protect and enhance the light in a painting. Perhaps the human soul is not dissimilar? Shadow prepares the eye for light just as light models the form of the shadow. Isn't that the whole concept of knowledge?"

"You believe then that knowledge is a good thing?" said Katherine. "In my experience it's been anything but. Wasn't it the discovery of knowledge that led to everything going wrong? I don't think I would have tempted Adam. It's much better usually not to know."

"Perhaps the tree of knowledge either kills you or makes you stronger. What do you think, Rowan?"

"It's in the nature of life to provide knowledge. What after all is experience if not knowledge?" said Rowan.

"There you go. But then maybe men are different. Do women want knowledge or are they just after sensation?" asked Jared with a mischievous twinkle.

"Sensation though is surely also a kind of knowledge," said Katherine.

"Perhaps women need to feel something is true whereas men try and talk things into being true?" said Rowan, feeling he was gallantly coming to Milena's mother's rescue. For a response she threw him another glance of ill-disguised disdain.

Over the past few weeks he and Milena, naturally drawn to one another, had struck up a flourishing cocoon-like intimacy. Every time a door opened he hoped to see her appear. Wherever he spoke to her, even inside a smoky nightclub, he felt they were underneath stars. There was something about her which restored everything to the exuberance of its original colour and meaning. Being with her felt as natural and heartening as binding sheaves of corn in an open field or pulling water up from a well. Lately though he had begun to notice that Milena flinched and recoiled at the approach of his hands. For him their relationship had entered the emotionally wrought phase where every little detail discloses the shadow of an obstacle. He was beginning to succumb to the idea that there might be a moment which if not grasped would fill with water like an imprint of a foot in the sand and slowly be erased.

At four in the morning, having drunk too much in a nightclub and undulating to left and right as if tossed about by a tide, Rowan and Milena entered Piazza della Signoria. They were alone and there was a roused expectant quality about the laid bare square and its history.

"Look at all the violence perpetrated against women," said Milena, pointing at the frozen footlit mythological figures under the loggia.

"You can be like Medusa, turning me to stone with a just look in your eye. Sometimes it's like Florence is telling us a story about our own lives. Don't you feel that?"

"I've got to take these shoes off. They're killing my feet."

Holding onto Rowan for support, Milena removed her shoes.

"Where are the stars tonight? Why aren't they guiding us? They should be guiding us. Don't you think of them, the stars, as silent witnesses?"

"Who is the more drunk, do you think, you or me?"

"I wish I could remember the first time I heard you speak," he said, dropping to his knees and kissing her hand. "It's always impossible to find that memory of anyone, isn't it? It's strange for me to realise I once heard my mother speak. And my father. Perhaps your father will like me better than your mother did. What do you think?"

"My father," she said and didn't finish the sentence.

"Be careful you don't step on any glass," he said, looking down at her bare feet.

"I'm always careful," she said, fanning out her skirt by clasping it at either side and treading on the tips of her toes like a ballerina. "I'm bored of being careful."

"When we get home, I'm going to wash your feet."

It suddenly began to pour with rain. Rowan took Milena's hand and ran singing with her across the piazza.

The sound of the rain and the refreshed smells it drew from the stones and evergreen foliage outside was sifted in through an open window near a table on which pollen-dusted wild orchids arched out of their vase. On a darkened pane drops of rain slid like quicksilver down the glass. Milena lit three candles. Fearing the spell might be broken at any moment, Rowan went to fill a bowl with water.

"Lift up your arms," he commanded. Brushing the alcove of her armpits with his fingers, he pulled her sodden black jumper inside out up over her head. Wisps of black lace supported her small breasts; the gentle swell of her stomach disappeared down inside the waistband of her skirt. Her wet hair, dyed burgundy with long blonde streaks, fell over her bare tanned shoulders.

Rowan knelt at her feet on a rug of blurred red and white symbols over which the flame of a candle played and thought how close this was to an act of imagination. He took her left foot and placed it in the warm water.

"You've got beautiful feet," he said.

"I hate my feet," she said.

"You've got beautiful ankles too."

"I don't mind my ankles, but I hate my feet."

He soaped off the deposit of dirt on her heel, watching his hands through which his will sought to convert her into an incandescent flame of yearning. He noted with gratification that she had closed her eyes.

"The left foot apparently is the female foot," he said. "The right foot leads and the left foot follows."

"Are you sure?"

"Let's see," he said and pulled her to her feet. Face to face, their eyes met in a shock of recognition. The increased pressure of her fingers on his waist confided a trail of fire through his still damp clothes. Rowan was the first to lower his eyes, to the wet footprints she had left on the rug. When he looked up again he found her mouth with his mouth and closed his eyes. The rising warmth of her body thickened the intimacy of the air. Rowan opened his eyes and looked over her naked shoulder and saw them both pearl pale reflected in the dark depths of a mirror. He unclasped her skirt and watched it fall to the floor around her ankles. Long strands of her rain-tousled hair trailed over his shoulder as her body quickened in kinship under his hands. Confident now she would not succumb to any misgiving he dropped down to his knees and helped her step out of her skirt. Finding the secret place in the inside hollow of her thigh with his mouth he slipped just the ends of his fingertips inside the black lace and gently traced a slow circle around the girth of her navel.

23

"Can we talk about what happened?" said Milena hurriedly. She had followed Rowan out into the corridor of the studio where they were alone. The note he had hoped to hear in her voice was decidedly absent. "The thing is," she said, sitting next to him at a significantly repelling distance, "I don't remember what happened. I was so drunk that it's all a blur in my head. I don't even remember walking home."

"If you don't remember," he countered, "how do you know you walked home? Perhaps I carried you."

"Did you?"

"Do I look like I could carry you?"

"I just want to clear things in my head. I hate getting so drunk I can't even remember what happened."

"So you're saying you don't remember me washing your feet or what happened afterwards?"

"You washed my feet?" Her incredulity was so badly acted, so self-consciously and studiously over-rehearsed that Rowan had no choice but to wonder if she took him for an idiot. He stared hard at her - to break down the sham of her performance? But her body remained rigidly unresponsive and her eyes whose lids were smudged with thumbprints of lilac dust refused to meet his on any terms save denial. He looked at her hands, the beautiful slender hands that had left their perspiring prints on his naked back less than twenty-four hours ago; her right hand clutched her bag so fiercely that the strain whitened her knuckles.

"So everything is to be swept under the carpet," he said.

"I don't even know what everything is. But no, I don't want to sweep under the carpet. I just want to get things straight in my head."

"Perhaps this is something which cannot be got straight in the head? Why not try feeling for once?"

"What do you mean?"

"At the moment I feel like I'm talking to a piece of furniture. How about if you actually started living inside yourself a little more? If you're not going to feel how are you going to know what to think? Isn't it in the nature of feeling to evolve thought? It's difficult to work out in you what's an idea and what's a feeling. In most people one gives way to the other; in you it's like there's an expanse of crisp snow between the thought and the feeling with no footprints one might follow. Anyway, what about the conversation we had afterwards?"

"What conversation?" she said obtusely as if clutching for protection some shard of forbidding ice within her breast.

"Whether or not you remember what happened has become superfluous; the fact is it's clear you don't want to remember which of course is not very flattering to me."

"It's got nothing to do with you. It's simply that..."

"What do you mean it's got nothing to do with me? It's as much my experience as yours even if that's obviously not how you choose to see it. Am I to just sit here and wait for you to tell me what the experience did or didn't mean?"

"Perhaps this is not the best place to talk," she said and, as if at her summons, the door of the oval room opened and Algernon Duff emerged, carrying a tattered paperback and as ever wearing his grime-encrusted cowboy hat.

"Sorry to interrupt your diminutive symposium chaps but I'm absolutely gasping for a smoke and I need to check some details for my Alexander lecture." Milena moved further away from Rowan to make space for Algernon between them.

Rowan never quite knew what to say to the third person and resented them always for making him feel at a loss. For him three was always a crowd. Algernon who peppered his dialogue with old English idioms and whose voice in its airy piping quality and frequent high-pitched squeals of exuberance was like some primitive wind instrument irritated him. As Rowan got up to return to his task of posing, a student called Faye Morgan arrived. She was carrying a huge package bound in brown paper and secured with string.

"I say, that's positively a leviathan of a parcel you have there, Faye. Could one be so bold as to inquire what's inside?" asked Algernon, taking off his hat and scratching his scalp.

"Swan's wings," said Faye. "I thought I was going to get stopped at customs. It's illegal you know to bring swans out of England."

"Even their vivisected bits?" Algernon was agog.

In the backroom Jared was painting a sketch of Tara as the Holy Virgin while Julian and Costanza were working on their study of the angel announcing the Holy Birth to the three shepherds. Faye opened her elaborate package and everyone beheld a huge pair of swan's wings.

"Oh Swami, aren't they beautiful," said Costanza, her face flushed with excitement.

"I don't suppose you know the story of Perceval and the swan?" asked Jared. "I think he accidentally shoots a swan and there's a beautiful passage about him becoming mesmerised by three red spots of blood in the virgin snow."

Julian, caressing the white fleece, shook his head.

"So, Julian, you've acquired a bigger pair of wings," quipped Jared with a mischievous light in his eyes.

"What do you mean, Jared?"

"The swallow becomes a swan. Swallow, swan, swami," said Jared. "Always the S and then the W."

"Like sword. Have I told you about my recurring dream in which I'm stabbed by a sword? I think it relates to a past life."

"Past lives and dreams - how can you really believe in all that stuff?" countered Jared. "Do you know what one of the last things Diane said to me was? She said, we'll meet again in another life. She said, maybe I'm no longer the man for her in this life but I'll always be her husband in eternity. Isn't that a rather too easy loophole?"

"I think you should try to talk to her," said Costanza. "I think..."

"I will never again talk to her," interrupted Jared. "That's the only power I have left - the power of silence. When she left me she lost all right to claim me as a friend."

Costanza lowered her eyes. Since his wife had left, Jared was more prone to these tempests of rage. It took often only a minor inconvenience or a flippant rejoinder to spark them off as if all the time some volatile subtext, hidden to all but himself, was reeling through his mind.

"I'm fed up with all these new-age beliefs," continued Jared, turning his back on everyone. "Aren't they all a justification for giving into ego? Christianity isn't about ego. It's about renouncing ego. Before the betrayal, Christ gave away bread and wine. That seems to me an incredibly powerful archetypal statement. You might worship an elephant god but what about Kali, Julian? Kali is the goddess of destruction. She demands human sacrifice."

"Without destruction there would be no creative act," said Julian, who had never once in his life found any need of anger to dramatise his inner life. "By the way, Jared, I'd love to do the Archangel Michael." He turned his inscrutable blue eyes on Jared. "I've told you about Supramannon, haven't I? He was what you might call our patron saint at the monastery. He in many ways is an Eastern equivalent of the Archangel Michael. He too is armed with a lance. At the monastery we had an image of Supramannon made of seven metals and during ceremonies it would emanate blue flames and sparks. It was my job to libate it and for healing processes it would be struck with a rod and produced this amazing spiritual note."

Jared tucked in his chin and tightened his brow. "So you want to do the vanquishing of Satan?"

"You can't vanquish the devil, Jared; no matter how many times you overcome him he will return in a new shape or guise."

"Oh, I forgot to tell you, Ewan has hired a German tramp to pose for him in the sculpture room. We should go down and take a look at him during the break. Ewan says he looks exactly like God in Titian's *Assumption*. How's that for a synchronicity? Or what is it you call synchronicities, Costanza?"

"Synchronosities," said Costanza.

24

As Katherine passed the church of Santa Trìnita the wooden door opened invitingly and a couple emerged, a pair of young lovers. The fleeting glimpse given of the interior of the church and its evocation of restful shadow attracted her, and on a whim she entered the cavernous house of prayer which embraced her in what amounted to a womb-like intimacy.

She sought to recall if she had ever visited this church before. Her memory now often played tricks on her. So much effort had she made in sealing off whole segments of it that in the process she had lost access to other connecting corridors and vaults. She fingered the pearls her mother had given her as an eighteen-year-old debutante which lay cool and impervious on her collar bone. Her heels echoed her decisive steps towards the right transept of the church, though only she knew what a sham this miming of assured self-possession was. She was not endowed with courage; she lacked the convictions which even made courage necessary.

She stopped at a chapel on whose walls she remembered now were frescoes of St. Francis. She *had* been here before. Reclaimed knowledge diffused shafts of light in the backwaters of her memory. She remembered a story of how St. Francis had brought back to life a small child, but not who had recounted it to her; she also remembered the kneeling figure of a quietly exalted woman she supposed to be the boy's mother. The machine which gave light rejected her coin three times. Then Ghirlandaio's *Adoration of the Shepherds* became a mirage of molten colour before her eyes. Its effect was to take her further back into the dispossessed archives of her memory. The image of the baby reminded her of the birth of Milena - the living, evolving and potentially treacherous repository of all her lies and guilt. She remembered physically the difficult birth and then looking into the prematurely-born baby's eyes and asking herself if this ugly wrinkled creature would grow up to be her enemy and her undoing. As her eye wandered over the painting the light shuddered off, eliciting in her a nervous stirring in that part of her body where the act of creation took place. She had also deceived her husband. Alex still had no idea Milena was not his child.

Now she could locate the church in time. It had become for her a place of remembrance. There was, she realised, a tomb here of a cardinal who bore a resemblance to her father. This time the light came on at her command and she stood over the marble repose of a long narrow face with deeply ingrained wisdom lines around his mouth, a mouth, she believed, that would have found its natural line in life in a faint ironic smile.

We assimilate people through their physical movements and gestures, she thought thinking of the way her father used to stoop over things. You, father, were your hands - nervous obsessive sensitive hands you had; always uncertainly fumbling the things you picked up as if you doubted your ability to firmly grasp anything for more than a fleeting moment. Katherine ran her fingers over the marble cheeks of the dead bishop and as she did so felt a chilling idea of death seep into her bloodstream, an idea that in her mind became an endless mounting landscape of snow into which she could almost feel her feet sinking. This cold neutral embrace which she had thought of as death she realised was her life. She was a law unto herself, unopposed, unrestrained, isolated. It occurred to her how necessary it was to thaw this unechoing winter habitat. A ring of fire was called for, the friction of two sharp edges coming into contact.

Looking to her left she saw the wooden statue of Magdalene.

Flat-chested, wizened, she still nevertheless held her vessel of consecrated oil; she still possessed, despite her haggard drained features and brittle body, the female's power to heal. Supposing though, a voice whispered, the vessel is now empty? I'm not that old, she protested. There had always been in her, she acknowledged, a perverse inclination to sabotage any pleasure she felt before it could fully take hold of her. Magdalene, by all accounts, had experienced life on her skin, had felt life with the whole of her body, and Jesus, when all was said and done, had warmed to her. Something in her rose up against this mean-spirited depiction of Magdalene and yet she could not deny the image possessed an immense hypnotic power.

Katherine noticed Magdalene's long claw-like hands which by contrast reminded her of Milena's hands whose elegant length and beauty always drew an emotional response from her. Where did she get those hands? Not from her certainly. From Max then. She could not remember what Max's hands looked like, the hands that had torn from her clothes while she was in an unconscious state. Was I always in an unconscious state back then? she asked herself. A harsh knife-sharp insistence on honesty now compelled her to interrogate herself as never before. Could I, should I have acted differently? Was it wrong to keep this cancerous lie sealed up in me all these years? Isn't it more the lie than the outrage itself that has conditioned my life? I should tell Milena the truth, she suddenly thought.

She was walking towards the fountain in Piazza Santo Spirito when she saw Damien Sparks outside the Cabiria bar.

"Just the person I wanted to talk to," he said, his left eyebrow arching up towards the map of wrinkles on his forehead. "You don't look terribly pleased to see me," he added.

"I'm not."

"I've made what I believe to be a rather extraordinary discovery. Or it would be if it actually verifies itself. You see, at present I'm working on a strong hunch."

"I'm not interested in your hunches, Damien."

"But supposing I was to say, it's my belief that Max Ashworth's son is here in Florence. You remember he had a son?"

That boy Rowan, Katherine thought, edging towards the fountain. I knew there was something familiar about him just as there was something familiar about my dislike of him. Three orange fish were ruffling the surface of the water in the fountain's basin. One makes a decision, she thought, and suddenly circumstances begin conspiring to bring it to fruition. I don't think Milena has slept with him. A mother can often tell these things. I remember asking myself that very question at dinner when I saw them talking together. And then Jared asked me if I saw a physical resemblance between the two of them.

"Are you listening to me? You look as though you've gone into a fourth dimension."

"I'm in a rush. Goodbye, Damien."

So it came about that Katherine, speaking clearly and adhering to facts as if standing in the dock, told her daughter the circumstances of her birth. To Milena her mother's words opened a deep trench in her being; her every word jarred with reverberations as if in her mind a heavy primitive tool was repeatedly striking a hollow piece of metal. The excavation site in Cephalonia came back to her; she saw herself down on her knees in the deep gash in the earth scraping away the rocky soil, helping with her discoveries to piece back together a coherent story of the past. Then she had enjoyed the novelty and excitement of breaking with all her old habits; now, forced down on her knees to piece back together her own life, she missed those habits as if they contained the seed of all her happiness, all her strength.

"The other thing is that this boy Rowan you're seeing is possibly the son of the man who raped me. In other words, it's possible he's your half-brother. I did notice some resemblance. There's no proof of course but Damien Sparks who was here at the time seems convinced of the fact."

"But Rowan has told me all about his family."

"Well, perhaps he's lying. After all, I should know how tempting it is to lie when the truth only fills you with shame. You haven't slept with him, have you? Milena? Did you hear what I said?"

From where Milena sat any horizon she might have seen was restricted by a temporary structure of corrugated iron on which posters of candidates in a forthcoming election advertised themselves. Beyond this crude palisade faint sounds of movement could be heard from the riverside creating the impression that she and Rowan were cut off from a hidden source of energy.

"Waking up with your naked back close to my mouth for me was as beautiful as life gets; now you tell me it was just a horrible mistake. Where does that leave me?" he said without raising his eyes. She made him feel like he was a sulking little boy thrashing with a stick at the surface of a lake trying in vain to create waves.

She frowned momentarily and then said in an airy and flippant tone designed to jar, "I can't help what I feel. I was drunk; you were drunk. It was a mistake. Can't we go back to how things were before?"

"What's the point of anything happening if the next day it's denied integration?" he said. "I'm accused of being cynical but isn't that the most cynical approach to life possible - to deny it meaning, depth and concatenation?"

"What's concatenation?" she said, irritated.

"A sense of a thread running through events which links them and gives them meaning. Supposing though it's not so much a question of what you do or do not feel as what you allow or do not allow yourself to feel?"

"I don't understand," she said giving him another one of her blank looks.

"Do you want to understand though? There's never any response of feeling in you."

Milena got angrily to her feet and walked off leaving Rowan, disliking himself, to finish his glass of red wine alone.

25

An entire restaurant, Osteria dei Benci, had been taken over to celebrate Rowan's birthday. Despite having entered into a cold war standoffishness with Milena, Rowan had decided at the last moment to invite her. He was disappointed that she had no gift for him and as a result he placed Vivienne and Costanza on either side of him while Milena drifted off to the far end of the table and found a seat between Algernon Duff and Andrew Hayward-Salt.

"Thank heavens you didn't invite Damien," said Vivienne. The wine glass she held bore the smudged red imprint of her painted lips.

"I've heard he's in love with you," said Rowan.

"Love?" she said screwing up her face in scorn. "To know love one has to have feelings and Damien has only motives. He enjoys messing with my mind."

"Just for the sake of it?"

"I have no idea because there's so little in him that I recognise as being human. The grotesque irony is that he's got under my skin in a way nobody else ever has - which doesn't of course say much for my susceptibilities." She sat tearing pieces off the brown paper table mat and screwing them up into ugly little nuggets. "By the way I'm very flattered to be your guest of honour despite the rather cutting looks I keep getting from Milena. Have you two argued? I mean, you were inseparable for a while. I was jealous of your relationship. The way you'd just sit in a corner and talk for hours. The two of you made everyone else feel utterly superfluous. Now all of a sudden she's been demoted to the boorish end of the table."

"Andrew's there. I thought you liked him."

"Only as a showroom dummy. One can dress him up in whatever one wants but I could never kiss him." They both looked over at Andrew; he, in common with Milena, was smiling at something Algernon Duff was saying. "I ought to warn you," said Vivienne pulling her long hair down over her breast, "that Algernon rather likes Milena."

"Isn't he still going out with Siobhan?"

"No. She still sleeps with him when she doesn't have a good book to read but she refers to him now in the past tense."

"He's such an old windbag," smiled Rowan.

"Why does Florence attract so many people who can't bear not to have the last word? Perhaps it's because Florence itself doesn't answer back the way London does. It's easier to covet illusions here. That said, now I'm about to leave, I've come to appreciate Florence. I was sceptical when I arrived."

"I remember."

"I had no desire to live in the past. And the past was all there seemed to be here. But I was living then as if there's no more to life than willed adventures and unwilled accidents. I've realised here that, at some point, we're compelled to re-evaluate ourselves in relation to the past. You know, time present and time past are both present in time future and time future contained in time past."

Across the table Jared was locked in conversation with his muse who since the project arrived had no longer been posing for him as Eve but instead as the Virgin Bride. Jared missed the sight of her naked body and was keen to return to his Eve. If I get her face, he was thinking, it'll be a rather remarkable Eve - a generous bountiful Eve reaching for the apple, not with any deceit in mind but simply with healthy female curiosity.

During the meal a gypsy boy who was often to be seen bartering his roses in Florence's restaurants entered the osteria and greeted Jared whom he recognised from previous encounters. Often Jared had brought his wife a rose from this cheerful little boy. Jared carefully selected a white rose and cavalierly handed it to Tara.

"You notice I didn't give you a yellow rose," he said. "White today in honour of the arrival of the swan's wings and the Madonna."

"I say, can we have one of your ravishing roses over here," called out Algernon Duff from the other end of the table. Rowan watched as Algernon selected a yellow rose and handed it theatrically to Milena. Not to be left out Andrew Hayward-Salt brought a blue rose and, summoning an even more theatrical flourish, handed his to the beautiful Blanche Phelps-Lang.

Jared now stood up and demanded silence.

"Who can remember the first lines of Dante's *Divine Comedy*?" he asked looking up and down the long wooden tables. "Algernon? You're our erudite scholar."

"Afraid not Jared, old chap. I could though if sufficiently cajoled recite the first lines of *Ozymandias*."

"Well, that's hardly appropriate. We're not here to celebrate an act of hubris and subsequent fall from grace. Is Ozymandias a hero of yours or just your party piece?"

It was Siobhan, piping in before Algernon had a chance to defend himself, who knew Dante's opening lines by heart which she recited now. "*Nel mezzo del cammin di nostra vita mi ritrovai per una selva oscura che la diritta via era smarrita.*"

"Dante was exiled from this city," Jared said, "and it's on the subject of exile that I want to speak. We all know about the perilous siege, or at least some of us do. The perilous siege was the seat at the Round Table which forcibly ejected unworthy knights. Its significance derives from the seat vacated by Judas when he realised his betrayal was known to Christ. Some might say the city of Florence works on a similar principle. That the city itself is a kind of perilous siege. Florence is often an idea we have to live up to. One also might say Florence is a kind of purgatory where one is called upon to acknowledge and address one's flaws, both artistic and spiritual. In many ways, Florence puts us to the test. And if we fail that test, Florence spits us out.

"As you all know we've been offered an opportunity to paint five large paintings for the apse of a church in Alabama. The bishop wants us to put the woman in the sky. How about that, Siobhan? What do you think about the idea of putting the woman in the sky?"

"I'd rather have my feet on the ground, Jared," said Siobhan. "I enjoy my bodily functions."

Everyone laughed.

"The question now arises, are we equipped both spiritually and artistically to undertake such a project?"

"Of course we are," interposed Julian with his thumbs hooked behind the straps of his brown dungarees.

"So, getting back to my theme, let's remember that Florence is a city of exile. However, I speak not of those who were exiled from Florence but instead those of us who have been exiled to Florence. Therefore I'd like to propose a toast. To Rowan and his exile."

At the end of dinner everyone began to swap places at the long table while the handsome Florentine waiters sat down at another table and ate their supper. Tara, Jared noticed, had gone to sit next to Ewan while his back had been turned. For a moment he had an empty place next to him. The table was littered with overflowing ashtrays and dirty plates. A wave of desolation passed through him. He felt as though he was standing alone on tidal flats of sand after sunset, the sense of departed life re-enforced by the lacklustre tattoo of withdrawing waves. Sometimes now it was his hands that remembered Diane. The feel of certain parts of her body was always latent on the tips of his fingers as a living memory. In the midst of life we are in death, he thought, for what had his wife done if not killed him? Everything Jared turned to now led back to something that was wanting in him, something dark against the light of his commands.

The restaurant's waiters took everyone to a nightclub nearby. The studio girls were writhing about on the dance floor like snakes trying to slough off a dead skin. Infrared light and scouring strobes reduced figures to bloodless spectres of themselves. Several times one of the girls came over and tried in vain to entice Rowan to join them on the dance floor. Milena was ensconced in an ever-more snug intimacy with Algernon in a secluded corner of the club. She had still not wished him a happy birthday. He watched her moisten her lips with the gloss he knew the scent of so well. Not once did she look his way though he could tell she was aware of his presence. Was she purposefully trying to make him jealous? That though, apart from having no precedent, did not make sense. Such a huge part of his nature was to run shy of what in his mind he convinced himself he wanted that for all he knew it was possible he misread everything. He still though believed that sooner or later she would come over and speak to him and so was shocked when she and Algernon got to their feet and left the club together.

The wooden crosses marking the stations of the Cross ushered Rowan up steps softened by pine needles towards San Miniato. It was five in the morning and Rowan had decided to watch the sunrise from the heights above the city. He sat with his back leaning on the closed metal gates of the Romanesque church. Behind him the grey-green and white marble façade and its mosaic of Christ gleamed through the slowly withdrawing darkness. An intermittent smell of laurel leaves spiced the early morning air and he noticed the glowing ethereal undertones in the sky beneath which Giotto's tower and the Duomo - the thrusting male line and the soft female curve - were drawn out more clearly than he had ever seen them and seemed to float as if loosened from the laws of gravity. The male and the female reconciled in harmony, he thought bitterly.

He had dreamed of Milena last night; he had sculpted her out of wet mud and leaves in the hushed tangled heart of a forest. He had crushed red berries in the palm of his hand to emulate the shyness of her wide mouth and taken the dew from stalks to help smooth the curves of her girlish body. He had remade her from the materials at hand to pose her a question. What is it in me that makes you run away? Feeling in him was forever trying to attach itself to an idea of action. Feelings after all are like waves and require a shore to break on.

The sky was now a virginal blue translucence as though bereft for a moment of the effects of both light and darkness. Then a crimson streak smouldered over the outline of the hills, a sinuous simmering bloodline. Rowan twirled the silver ring round and round on his finger. I'm a coward, he thought. Should not life be adventure? Should not it have a transfiguring quest at its heart? Florence was where he had come to discover his heritage. Now he was here, he always seemed to err on the side of caution, prevarication, taking tomorrow for granted. Rowan felt he was drifting idly towards knowledge; lacking though was some central catalytic agent which might not only balance the sway of opposing forces but implement them in action. His body was coursed with veins through which blood and water ingeniously performed their cycles; why was not the life of his mind equally as efficacious? A single anxious thought could still flood his entire being with devouring darkness. He stared for a moment at the glowering rim of the sun rising over the line of hills to his right. Then he noticed an old man with dishevelled white hair limp slowly along the road at the bottom of the steps. Something about the man fascinated Rowan. He tried to imagine what he might have to say for himself and was tempted to go down and ask him a question. The man looked up at Rowan and they exchanged glances. Then he disappeared behind the oak trees of the viale.

26

Cycling two abreast, Jared and Tara followed the river as far as the Cascine and there entered a withdrawn world of lawns and trees which extended over vast acres. Tara had brought a picnic lunch, and far away from the centre's exhaust fumes and tour parties, they sat down by the river. Tara began passing Jared things she pulled out of brown paper bags - bread, pecarino cheese, sun-dried tomatoes, olives, prosciuto.

"Something strange happened to me the other day," said Jared when they had finished eating. "Before setting up my easel I decided to visit the church I'm painting. I was alone when I entered the crypt. There was one alabaster window - alabaster which refracts a diffused glow rather than letting through light. However, there was a chink in the window through which a thread of light entered the vault. I saw that the golden lance was striking a tiny cross a wayfarer had incised on the altar; it wavered there like a butterfly."

"That sounds amazing. I wish I had seen it."

"But what does it mean, do you think? These signs appear to us, like oracles, but the meaning behind them is often mystifying. Do you believe in signs, that we're being guided from outside in some way?"

"I think it's a possibility."

"But you're not religious?"

"My father calls me a pagan."

"Tell me about your upbringing. I had a very strict upbringing, you know. But it was a different culture back then. I guess it was the sixties that changed everything. Your father's a sixties guy, right?"

She smiled.

"And he's never quite recovered?" he joked. "Still wandering about trying to find Nirvana? Julian is a sixties guy too though he seems much younger. Tell me, what do you think of Julian and Costanza?"

"I think they're both lovely."

"But don't you say that about everyone?" Jared teased, playfully waving his forefinger at her.

Disclosing the interior of her mouth, her white teeth, her red tongue, Tara took another healthy bite of her red apple. "I mean it though," she said with an overflow of the fruit's juice faintly moistening her fleshy lips. "That's what I feel."

"What about their relationship together?"

"They always seem completely committed to each other. You can tell they really love each other."

"Costanza was very young when she met Julian. Probably he's completely formed her. The problem then is, women change. That's what happened with Diane. She always professed herself *lunatique*. That means changeable in French, like the moon. But tell me more about yourself."

"I've never quite met the right person. Once or twice I thought I had."

"The French chef? Weren't you studying French when you first arrived?"

"That's all over. He's gone back to his wife. On a cruise liner you get bored easily. That's where I met him. I was working as a waitress."

"You shouldn't embark on affairs just because you're bored." Jared smiled but he meant what he said.

"It was a bit more than that. I do seem to have this pattern of falling for married men."

"How many married men have there been then?"

"Only two, but even so I've recognised a familiar pattern."

"We all have patterns in our lives. The question is, can we break them? My wife certainly never broke hers. Nietzsche said that everything repeats itself in endless wheels. But do things just repeat themselves in the same forms? There's always the trickster element; there's always some twist the next time round. Some say we inherit our patterns from our parents. I suppose that's the idea of the father visiting his sins upon his children, though I would imagine that this holds equally true for mothers as well. I have a very loving mother. She's always supported me in everything I do. I sometimes think that's been my problem."

"What do you mean?"

"Well, she's laid a precedent. Because of her, I expect all women to be generous and supportive. What do you think? Do our parents create our patterns or do they have a more mystical source?"

"I can see that our parents create our patterns. I think I always have to see something of my father in a man to find him attractive. It's never obvious and sometimes I don't even realise the similarities until afterwards but it is as if I'm trying to complete or continue my dad somehow through my boyfriends."Tara twirled her kaleidoscopic bangles round and round on her wrist.

"What about the guys at the studio?" he inquired. "There are some pretty eligible males knocking about."

"Like who?"

"Like...I don't know. Like Rowan, for example," he said.

"I don't think Rowan likes me very much. Anyway, he's not at all my type. He's too analytical. I always get the feeling he's privately criticising me."

"Rowan is critical, isn't he? When he first arrived in Florence he hardly spoke and never smiled. Florence has done him good though. Except he is too critical. What about Ewan then? After all, it was he who brought you here and you certainly seem to get on well."

"Ewan's very easy to get on with. He's very easy-going like me."

"He's not at all like me. And then he's apparently having an affair with Tim Garnett's daughter Beatrice."Did the muscles around Tara's mouth momentarily stiffen or had he imagined it?"Ewan's had quite a lot of success at my studio. He was here three years ago, you know. Despite his thinning hair - or perhaps because of it - he does seem to hold an attraction for females."

Tara smiled and then poured them both out more water into their plastic cups.

"This, you know, is where Shelley wrote his *Ode to the West Wind*," said Jared, nodding over his shoulder towards the deserted park.

Oh, lift me as a wave, a leaf, a cloud!
I fall upon the thorns of life! I bleed!
A heavy weight of hours has chained and bowed
One too like thee: tameless, and swift and proud.

Blood had come to his face while he recited the familiar lines and an impassioned inward-looking light intensified the charge of his blue eyes. When he turned now to Tara, she was look-ing at him with a smile that parted her lips a fraction. By reflex he parted his own lips, and his right shoulder dipped almost imperceptibly towards the girl; his body's wish, not facilitated by any response, was abolished by some nagging doubt in his mind. The next thing he knew the moment had passed and Tara was rummaging in a brown paper bag.

"That's my favourite poem in the whole of English literature. Do you know it?" he asked, lowering his eyes.

"I think I read it at school," Tara said, unpeeling an orange.

In a mercurial glitter of reflected sunlight, a swan came glid-ing downstream towards them. Jared thought of the preserved wings of the dead bird they had used to paint the wings of angels in the studies, then remembered the bird Diane had painted abducting her in the last picture she did before leaving him. This though, unlike the grotesque bird his wife had painted, was a living creature, sublime in its beauty and pulsing grace.

27

In honour of Rowan's last supper with the family, Tim had composed a witty poem which the youngest son Roland read out after Rachel had appeared bearing a cake. Rowan would, he knew, miss the rich purring intimacy of the home - even though in the midst of its vibrant enfolding pulse his overriding desire was often to make excuses and return to the solitude of his room. Why was he always so eager to escape from the pressure of having to give any kind of account of himself? Only the beautiful female, he realised, lured him out of his hermetic sanctuary into the world of oppositions.

After dinner he went upstairs to pack. He opened the drawer of his desk and pulled out a small wad of photos. Many of them were of the Thanksgiving dinner in the oval room at the studio. He studied more closely than ever before his only photo of Milena who had returned to the excavations in Greece. No longer able to take her for granted, the face that met his eyes in the photo had had mystery restored to it. He saw her again as she walked away from him the last time, in her long lilac skirt, and the image seemed to mark some cherished lonely outpost in his feeling for life. We were both too shy with each other, he thought. Rowan experienced the hurt of her dismissive gesture all over again and was about to tear the photo in half when a wiser voice stopped him. Then there was a knock at his door and Beatrice entered.

"I've brought you a present," said the willowy eldest daughter of Tim and Rachel. She was wearing a baggy old blue sweater and a floral skirt. She handed Rowan a book.

"The *Vita Nuova*," he said.

"You said you'd never read it so I thought..."

He kissed her on either cheek. She was more or less the same height as Rowan. She smelt faintly of some tender sweet herb.

"It's a nuisance this aunt is coming otherwise you could have stayed. How's the packing going?"

"Okay."

"We're all very sad you're leaving. You must come back and visit us."

Rowan was used to Beatrice showing off; she was both clever and flighty and as a rule flitted around rooms as diaphanously as her mind performed its butterfly dances over the fruits of her learning; tonight, she appeared more sober and statuesque and an awkwardness knotted the atmosphere in which anything said was liable to sound either shrill or flatly monotone.

"Why don't you take a break in your packing and come outside to look at the moon? It's beautiful tonight."

They stopped not far from an old fig tree. Huge black paw prints mingling with ragged white drifts made the sky look like an aerial map of the earth in the midst of which Rowan could even make out a slightly errant idea of England's land mass. The moon was almost full, though was missing a chunk along its southern circumference. It now drifted flirtatiously behind a black cloud.

"The moon shines bright," quoted Rowan. "On such a night as this, when the sweet wind did gently kiss the trees and make no noise..."

Beatrice turned to him with a look of fledgling wonder and without thinking he kissed her. Even while he was kissing her and his hand folded over her breast he was thinking how terribly, horribly wrong this was. He pulled away and by the light of the almost full moon saw and felt how offended Beatrice was in her female pride.

"The moon shines bright," he repeated but immediately realised how insensitive and stupid it was to pretend nothing had happened.

"I'm going to bed. Goodnight," she said with ice-cold disdain and walked off with long contemptuous strides towards the house.

He sat on the border of the unploughed field and thought about his life. I don't particularly want gratification from a woman, he thought. I want poetry and imagination. I want her to live in me as a beautiful idea. I want her to protect me from the banality and erosion of everyday life. And yet I'm close to no one. Is this why I'm still stumbling about the world like some half-grown fool? Snatching at uncorrelated kisses in the moonlight, uprooted from one temporary lodging to another?

He felt the hard earth suddenly reverberate and then saw as if in a dream two horses gallop past within six feet of him, a white mare and a chestnut mare. They were whinnying as they thundered off down towards the dark trees skirting the lake. The shock of the appearance of the two horses stayed with Rowan. It seemed charged with some cryptic significance. The white mare had playfully tossed its head while galloping past and Rowan had seen - he could still see it now - a laughing light in the animal's eyes. He wondered what Jared with his insistence on seeing life as a map of fateful symbols might have made of the appearance of the two horses. Jared was always urging him to re-read Dante. He remembered how on his arrival in Florence either Jared or his friend had compared him physically to the statue of Dante in Santa Croce. But tonight he had rejected Beatrice who had offered him the *vita nuova*.

He looked up at the almost full moon again. It had escaped from the clutches of the black clouds and was now shining down in a virginal clearing of pure blue-black sky. Rowan wondered what Milena was doing at this precise moment. More vivid and arresting than the photo, he saw an image of her in his mind's eye - she was smiling the way she did when he teased her - and he realised that she belonged to his blood; to the evolutionary imperative of his nature; she was a vital part of his indispensable belief that life had meaning.

The next day, a beautiful day, suspended between seed-time and harvest, a day of quivering gossamer threads and leaves struck translucent by sunlight, Rowan tramped across fields and vineyards. A few almond trees were in flower, the white flowers like snow blossoming from scarlet buds with tiny thumbprints of golden pollen on the anthers. The sun was warm on the back of his neck. He walked down into the valley and saw ahead what looked like an abandoned farmhouse. Approaching the broken arched gate of its garden he noticed a rusty plaque. He remembered having been here with Rachel at the beginning of his stay in Florence. The first name on the list of partisans murdered by the Nazis, meaningless when first he had seen the plaque, was Giuliana Cristalli.

He sat down on the ground and lit a cigarette. The sharp blades of grass he fingered seemed to throb in response to the sadness of what had happened here. Rowan tried to bring to life, add to it colour, the photo of Giuliana he had seen at the dance school. He looked around, at the wide sweep of valley and the cultivated slopes, to see what she had seen before the final darkness mounted up behind her eyes. He experienced her death as a strangely personal loss.

Rowan walked in a wide arc back towards the Garnett home. He was now within sight of the lake at the foot of the valley. He saw something moving about in the water and realised that someone was swimming there. Kira, he thought. She saw him at the moment he saw her and began languidly swimming towards him. She stopped not far from the shore.

"If you want to talk to me you'll have to come in the water."

"I can't swim. I've already told you that."

"You don't have to swim. Just come in up to your waist."

"The water must be freezing."

"Stop making excuses. How many times a day do you make excuses? For every excuse you make, some flame of vitality is extinguished in you," she said with a broad mocking smile. She then began splashing up water in his direction. "If you're not coming in I'm going to swim away and you'll never see me again."

"Why is it so important that I come into the lake?"

"I'm going to count to ten. *Uno, due, tre, quattro...*"

"How do I know you're not luring me to a death by drowning?"

"*Cinque, sei, sette...*"

"Okay."

He was aware of her watching him closely while he knelt down and took off his shoes and socks; he caught her eye and its mischievous twinkle while he undid his trousers and stepped out of them. The sharp nature of the terrain came up through the contact his bare feet made with the stony ground. Dressed now in a t-shirt and a pair of boxer shorts he felt self-conscious and helpless.

"I might keep my t-shirt on though," he said.

"No clothes," she said. "As naked as the day you were born."

He did as he was told and took his first steps into the lake. Almost immediately he was absorbed by the freezing murky water up to his thighs. The impact of it made him catch his breath.

"Why do you always hold everything back? If the water's cold yell out loud. Make a song and dance."

Immersion was his big fear. The thought of his head going under water was no less terrifying than the idea of death itself. He held out his arms as if to grab hold of a support in case of slipping. When the water had risen up to his waist he stopped and looked sheepishly over his shoulder to see how far he had waded from the safety of the shore.

"What exactly is the point of this? You've got me in the water, now what?"

"It's natural for you to be frightened. Why do men always try and conceal fear from women? Often that's what makes a man weak and silly - not the fear itself, but the urge to hide it."

"I'm not trying to hide it; I'm trying to overcome it."

"You should have more confidence in yourself, be more trusting. Why don't you come a little closer?"

"I'm not moving."

Rivulets parted from either side of her as she launched herself into fluid breast strokes. She swam in a circle around him, creating small waves which lifted the water up in eddies over his chest. When she came to a halt she was closer to him. He could see now the beautiful emerald green of her eyes, the strangely withheld sensuality suggested by the line of her lips.

"I'm leaving today," he said. He studied her features for a response. She looked at him quizzically, but he could detect no emotion.

"This might be the last time we see each other." She swam over to him and deftly slipped a hand to the back of his neck. "Now lift up your feet and let your legs float; I'll hold you up." She made a motion with her left hand to indicate how she would support him. Flashing drops slid down her breasts which were now exposed to the sunlight. "There's nothing to worry about. Unless you don't trust me?"

When he tentatively let himself fall back into her custody he felt her palm apply a light pleasurable pressure to the base of his spine. Reassured only in part he lifted first one foot and then the other; they dangled mistrustfully not far from the security of the bed of the lake. Kira applied more pressure to her support of his back.

"Lift a little higher," she said. "It's for your own benefit. Just see what it's like to let the water take your weight."

When he did as he was told she lithely and quickly withdrew both her hands and Rowan, clawing wildly at the water, disappeared beneath the surface. Kira had swum two or three strokes away and was looking at him with playful bemusement as he reappeared.

"You've just been baptised," she said swimming towards the far bank.

As he walked along Borgo San Jacopo, Jared saw Hans the German tramp settling down for the night outside the church. The bearded outcast who modelled at the studio slept on a gravestone beneath the Romanesque portico. Jared called out a greeting and the grizzled old man, drunk as usual, called back something, the only word of which Jared caught was "Tara."

Instead of taking his habitual route home, Jared continued along the river. In the distance, he could hear a girl's voice singing. Lights flickered on the black hills before him, and on the water of the river he noticed a smudged red reflection which never changed to green. In the diffused nimbus of a streetlamp two figures were locking their bikes outside the Serristori studio. He recognised them almost immediately as Ewan and Tara. The two tiny figures entered the building together and the door closed behind them.

Jared arrived to critique the work of his advanced students early at the Serristori studio the next morning. He noticed Tara's bike was still chained up outside the building, the bike he himself had given her. Cuckolded again, he thought. He remembered having lent Ewan his car one weekend. No doubt he had used it to drive Tara somewhere. On its restoration he had found a crumpled postcard under the seat. It was addressed to Ewan and featured a reproduction of a Roman statue of Priapus, that old fertility god with the outlandish genitals.

At a turning of the stairs as he made his way to the top floor of the palazzo he heard echoing footsteps above and, looking up, saw Tara coming down. Her features froze upon seeing him. He gave her a smile with disapproving knowledge in it and a rather curt greeting. Today, Thursday, was given over to his teaching responsibilities. He did not thankfully have to paint her.

After the weekly lecture there was a drinks party at Davina Fitzwilliam's flat opposite the Brancacci Chapel. As the evening wore on, Jared could not help but notice how possessive Ewan Slater was of Tara's company. They had been sitting close together on a sofa all night, advertising an exclusive complicity. Now and again, Jared caught Ewan's eye.

Julian and Costanza did not as a rule attend these parties held by the younger set and Jared found himself trapped into awkward conversations with students like Seamus and Davina around whom he was never quite able to relax. When Blanche came over he felt better - to look at the beautiful Blanche was always a pleasure. While they were discussing the last portrait she had painted there was a sudden uproar of ferocious snarling and growling. He looked up to see his dog baring its teeth at Ewan Slater.

"I stepped on his tail," said Ewan. "Not on purpose."

"*Attention*," said Jared in French to his dog. The dog cowered and looked up fearfully though appealingly at its master. "Can I have a quick word with you, Ewan?" Jared beckoned him over towards Davina's bedroom. They entered the room together and Jared closed the door behind them. The double bed was strewn with coats and jackets. Jared tossed them aside and sat down.

"I just wanted to congratulate you," he said.

Ewan looked blankly at his paymaster, teacher and landlord. "What for?"

"Tara's a lovely girl."

"Shouldn't you be telling her that rather than me?"

"So, what about Beatrice?"

"That's over," said Ewan.

"Just like that? Apparently Beatrice is rather upset. Apparently Beatrice feels rather used. You know her father is an old friend of mine? We go back a long way together. I've watched Beatrice grow up."

"I didn't instigate the thing with Beatrice. It was her who was throwing herself at me."

"And that makes you blameless?"

"I don't actually see that it's any of your business," said Ewan gruffly.

"Look here, you've taken advantage of an eighteen-year-old girl on my premises - that, you know, *is* my business. You swagger about and act all cool around my studio, but do you know what? You're just another spoilt trust fund kid. And you're here to pick the fruit from the tree. How many of my students have you bedded?"

"You can't stop people from sleeping with each other just because they attend your art school, Jared."

"I want you out of my studio. Your time here has come to an end. No more rich pluckings for Ewan Slater at my expense. I want you out of my studio."

Jared left the party, forgetting in his anger his dog.

"I think Ewan set me up," Jared was telling Julian in the backroom of the studio. "I think Ewan has a problem with his own father and used me as a scapegoat to get back at the male authority figure. You do not steal the maestro's muse. Do you think Van Dyck ever had his muse stolen by one of his assistants? Of course he didn't. Ewan is out because you do not rob Beatrice of her virginity or Apollo of his muse."

"Ewan seemed pretty upset when I saw him," said Julian. "He said he had been trying to call you all morning and even went round to your apartment last night."

"I knew it was him. I didn't answer the door or the phone. Let him squirm. But he's out of my studio. He's hit the perilous siege. I don't need Ewan Slater. And apparently he deflowered the fairy Kerrie too. Is that why I'm running a school - to provide vestal virgins for Ewan Slater?"

"Perhaps you ought to talk to him though?" said Julian.

"Oh you British, you always have to see the other person's point of view."

"Well, you may not think about this very often, Jared, but other people do happen to have a point of view." Julian smiled.

Before Jared could respond, Costanza walked over to him and rested a hand on his shoulder. "Jared, why do you care about her physical self? Look at the picture you've painted of her. You've painted a beautiful spiritual picture. And you've painted it with real love. That's been her real gift, to give you this picture."

Jared was moved by Costanza's words and averted his eyes to his picture of the Holy Virgin.

When later Tara arrived to pose Jared said with cold formality, "I'm going to work on the Magdalene picture today," He noticed that her attire was less careless than usual. A white cotton shirt open at the neck and a long thin skirt patterned with wildflowers suggested an effort on her behalf to appear more generously feminine.

"Do you know why I'm going to work on Magdalene?" he asked as he mixed a fierce vermilion on his palette.

Clutching the piece of wood which served as the cross, she shook her head.

"Because I'm not painting Ewan Slater's lover as my Madonna. In fact, I'll never touch that picture again. It's finished."

He looked down at his palette and dipped his brush in the little pot of medium. When he looked up again, preparing to march forward and lay down the day's first brushstroke, he saw that she was crying. She was trying hard to maintain the pose. Catching Jared's eye she broke down and left the room.

For a while he did not know what to do. Standing by his painted sketch of the Crucifixion in which Tara was both Magdalene and the Virgin he defended himself against the implied criticism of her tears but was also partly assuaged in his hurt by them. Finally he went out into the corridor. Tara with her head bowed was sitting by the window.

"Let's go back into my studio and talk," he said.

They sat down opposite each other in front of the Descent from the Cross.

"I admired you for your independence," said Jared.

"But I am independent. Me and Ewan are just friends really."

"What about Beatrice?"

"I didn't know anything about Beatrice until you told me by the river the other day."

Jared's harsh expression softened a little. At least he had delivered a wound to her.

"Beatrice is one hurt eighteen-year-old girl. Ewan took advantage of her and then dumped her. I don't call that very nice, do you?"

"No," said Tara.

"You haven't been very honest with me, either."

"I haven't been very honest with myself."

"Shall I tell you something? For six months we've seen each other more or less every day; for six months we've shared an intimacy of sorts - or not?"

She assented with a sad nod.

"Well, for six months you've been my wife," said Jared. "You've helped me take my mind off what my wife did to me."

She began to cry again and Jared lifted her out of the chair and took her in his arms. He ran his hand through her hair, sweeping it back from her brow. They remained in each other's arms until he kissed her paternally on the forehead and then they separated.

IV

Regnabo

29

Julian Swallow was kneeling forward over the old open fireplace and blowing at capricious orange sparks which as yet had refused to leap into flame and set alight the neatly stacked firewood.

"Did you learn to do that at your community?" asked Jared, rubbing his hands together against the fierce icy cold that rose up from the flagstones.

"I was always firestarter," said Julian.

The French farmhouse's every low doorway had to be negotiated with a timely stoop. The building no doubt dated back to the times of food famines and witchhunts. Its rough-hewn whitewashed stones were no less full of chinks and crevices inside than outside. No attempt had been made to hide or blend the huge heavy pine beams. They crisscrossed the ceilings like the skeleton of a structure still to be christened.

Everyone was sitting around the fire. A log now hissed and crackled and shot up a towering flame. Jared, leaning into the red glow to warm his hands, said,

"Can you pass me my Bible, Edward? I thought what we might do is paint a very subtle motif of water into the last two pictures - the Immaculate Conception and the Archangel Michael - which would be a reference to the flood. Here's the relevant passage in *Revelations: And there appeared a great wonder in heaven, a woman clothed with the sun, and the moon under her feet, and upon her head a crown of twelve stars: And there appeared another wonder in heaven; and behold a great red dragon, having seven heads and ten horns, and seven crowns upon his heads. And his tail drew the third part of the stars of heaven, and did cast them to the earth: and the dragon stood before the woman which was ready to be delivered, for to devour her child as soon as it was born.* Later we come to this passage: *And to the woman were given two wings of a great eagle, that she might fly into the wilderness, into her place, where she is nourished for a time, and times, and half a time, from the face of the serpent. And the serpent cast out of its mouth water as a flood after the woman, that he might cause her to be carried away of the flood."*

"You would have made a great pastor, Jared," said Edward.

Rowan, sitting in an armchair by the fire, had never before heard these passages from *Revelations* and was struck by how cryptically pertinent they were to his own mysterious origins. In the Bible, the woman had survived. But there had been no such salvation for his mother. She had gone under, she had been devoured by the raging waters. Why though, he wondered again, had his mother given him up for adoption *before* the flood which killed her.

Later they all drove into the nearby town of Uzés. As they crossed a bridge known as the Pont du Diable Jared noticed a signpost emblazoned with a name he had not seen for almost twenty years - Arpaillargues. Arpaillargues was the little town where he and his wife had spent the happiest year of their relationship.

"It's extraordinary how the past is always lying in ambush," he told Rowan as they arrived in the picturesque main square of Uzés where a market was being held. "The older I get the more I realise there is a logic to life, except it's a logic which will not quite make itself plain to our reason, if that makes sense."

"I think the past can lock the door to the future until we've understood it and to understand it we often have to imaginatively make it happen again," said Rowan, still thinking of his mother and the flood in *Revelations*.

As Jared was searching the various stalls for gifts to take back to his two daughters, he heard a familiar voice greeting him. He turned round and saw his old friend Frank.

"Jared! What the hell are you doing on my turf? And by god, if my eyes don't deceive me, it's Julian Swallow! Damn, I drew you twenty years ago in Florence. You haven't changed a bit!"

"*You* certainly have," smiled Julian. Frank gave him a hug; Julian was clearly embarrassed by such a tactile dramatisation of emotion.

"But what the hell are you guys doing in France? Have you finally seen the light, Jared? I always told you the French landscape is superior to the Italian."

Jared explained the circumstances of their visit and then took Frank aside.

"Did you hear about Diane?" he asked solemnly in the shade of a stall selling wildflowers and honey.

"No."

"She's left me, Frank; she's gone off with another man."

"Diane?" asked Frank incredulously. "But she loved you, Jared. She was crazy about you. Why, I remember when she was chasing you about all over Florence."

"Well, she left, Frank. Your marriage ended, and now my marriage has ended too."

"When did this happen?"

"Last year."

"Are you still hurting, Jared?" asked Frank and laid a hand on Jared's shoulder.

Lying alone in bed that night, Jared had no option but to contain in silence the day's disclosures. He saw Diane barefoot by the sea, laughing and kicking at the waves with the Mediterranean sun high in the sky above her bare shoulders; he saw Diane waiting for him beneath the crisp white sheets in a foreign hotel room, her clothes lying in a pile at the foot of the bed; he saw Diane standing on the summit of a hill, beckoning him to climb up through the bramble and briar to join her in her private sweeping vision. But he was unable to sustain any image of Diane in her best intentions now; every picture of her he possessed had been corrupted by one deed.

At six in the morning Jared was still awake. First, it was the sound of birdsong he heard enter his room, then a faint deep chanting. He assumed this was Julian, in the room next door, chanting at his small shrine. He tried to imagine the scene in detail but soon drifted into sleep. He was awakened no more than an hour later by a raucous cry from the courtyard down below. This too was Julian. At seven every morning Julian went down into the courtyard and performed a credible imitation of a peacock's cry to get everyone up for communal breakfast. The peacock being essentially a vain and ostentatious bird, Jared thought it odd that the ascetic Julian Swallow chose to imitate its rather irritating call.

After breakfast everyone went out in a convoy of cars to the spot they had chosen for their morning paintings. High on the ridge of a ravine Jared set up his easel. He had wandered as far as possible from the others though still felt himself under observation. He was uncomfortable with Julian's determination to marshal everyone into a tightly-knit unit, all painting within sight of each other. Jared, who always took an agonisingly long time to apply paintbrush to canvas, bemoaned a privacy denied him. The riverbed was almost dry; huge polished stones reflected the sun's glitter back up into the air.

His meeting with Frank had set him thinking about his artistic life. Jared had been trained by his teacher to see the whole shape. He could still hear the man's fey clipped New England accent as he delivered up his scathing rebukes and admonitions. "I'm the eye of the needle; all art history passes through me." The thought of his teacher brought a smile to Jared's lips even though his bitter stream of impeachments had done much to discourage his confidence in himself as an artist. Nevertheless, he often caught himself imitating his old teacher. In many ways he represented the most fateful encounter of Jared's life. What was it he had said? "It's far more important that you teach than become the greatest painter who ever lived - because if you don't pass on the knowledge I'm giving you it will die out." He had done what the eighty-year-old man asked of him. He had taught, he had passed on the knowledge. And, in the process, he had lost his wife.

Suddenly a series of explosions rang out whose echoes ricocheted hollowly down in the ravine. Up in the cerulean blue sky two birds of prey were obsessively circling. Before long, the sound of men shouting reached him, accompanied by what he now recognised as gunshots. He looked over towards Julian and Costanza who, lower down on the ridge, were closer to the source of the disruption. He scrambled down the slope to join them.

"It's a boar hunt," said Julian with marked disapproval. "Look, can you see down there? The men have goaded the boar into a corner."

Jared could see the hounded cowering animal. A group of men carrying guns were throwing stones at it. The stones tore red smudges from its dark fur. Repeatedly, it charged only to be struck and knocked off balance by another large stone. Finally, its legs collapsed. A man approached and crushed the wounded animal's head with a huge rock.

Costanza meanwhile had marched off with a look of horror on her face, followed by Julian. Jared turned to see Julian cradle his girlfriend in his arms.

"That was Cromagnon man," he said when Julian and Costanza returned to their easels. "We've just witnessed a ritual which dates back to prehistoric times. This is actually an incredibly primitive landscape."

"Guru can remember who he was in a previous life," said Julian, one of the eight people sitting at the table. Outside heavy relentless drops of rain splashed down through the fig leaves. The courtyard at the bottom of the ivy-shrouded stairs was an argument of churned up mud and unripe fallen fruit. "He was a rather famous monk. Even now pilgrims visit his grave. Guru always used to find that very amusing. Don't they realise that I've already come back? he used to say. I've seen a photo of this monk and the resemblance *is* remarkable. The community attracts quite a few people who can remember their past lives and as a result find it difficult to adapt to their present life."

Julian then went on to speak of a celebration of Shiva which took place on the Ganges while Jared, drinking wine and frequently refilling his glass, made little effort to conceal his scepticism. He did not agree when Julian spoke of all religions being essentially the same.

"Shiva's not Christ," protested Jared, his arms folded over his chest. "This isn't India. We've grown up with Christian beliefs, Christian images. You might turn your back on Christianity but that's our heritage."

"I respect all sacred places and all sacred images, Jared," said Julian firmly.

"Can we in the West really though believe in reincarnation?"

"Why do you always have to be so negative, Jared?" asked Costanza, an angry flush burning her cheeks. "To some people what we're doing - painting pictures - is nothing but decadent and spoilt behaviour. We're not helping anyone. Sometimes I think of the people who go to third world countries and devote themselves to looking after the poor and I feel ashamed of myself and my life."

"Like Julian saving all the ants?" said Jared, referring to an event yesterday when, having realised there was a nest in a piece of wood he had thrown on the fire, Julian retrieved the smouldering branch over which hundreds of ants scurried from the flames and restored it to the outside world. "Isn't it your vanity though, Costanza, to see yourself as a paragon of positive generous thinking? I try to create a criterion. I want to separate the good from the bad and the great from the good. I want to find the gold. I don't want to live in a world where everything's been flattened out. We've lost the high ground. Think of what the church once was - exalted architecture, exalted art and exalted music all combining to disclose the transfiguring realm of life. Isn't that the real way of helping mankind? Well, you go to India and feed your poor, Costanza. But I wonder now if you've learnt anything at my studio."

Jared got to his feet and left the room, leaving behind a crackling static of tension. The room he vacated had six windows, all of a different size and shape. On a round low table surrounded by a half-circle of flowery cushions, was an empty birdcage. Had the bird flown or simply died in captivity? The occupants of the room, each feeling the oppression of his or her own silence, did not quite know where to look, what to say. Edward, shuffling uncomfortably in his chair, was the first to speak. "This place gives me the creeps," he said. For the third time tonight the lights went out. The large room was diminished to a boundless darkness suffused by the hypnotic rippling red glow of the fire.

"It's getting difficult to know what to do about Jared," Costanza could be heard if not seen to say. "Swami tried talking to him yesterday. He took him aside after lunch and asked him what was wrong and Jared just smiled disdainfully and said, nothing's wrong, Julian. But it's obvious he's not happy. And he's infecting the whole house with his antagonism."

"The Tara-Ewan saga seems to have slightly unhinged him," said Rowan. "It was, I suppose, a rather grotesque caricature of what happened with his wife. Thus once again, his wife is looming large in his thoughts and there's a kind of tug-of-war between sadness and anger inside him which is never quite resolved."

"But he has to learn to respect boundaries," said Julian. "At some point in his life he has to get beyond anger as a response to what he doesn't like or what prevents him from getting his way. It's his way of refusing to think anything through to new knowledge. I've never met anyone with as much mental energy as Jared but neither have I ever met anyone who squanders so much energy by repeatedly going back over old ground. I thought bringing him here would relax him; instead he seems determined to turn us all into enemies."

"He's like King Lear though, isn't he?" said Rowan. "He's used to being obeyed. As far as he's concerned it's his royal prerogative."

"My suspicion is, he doesn't want to do this project. He doesn't feel he's up to doing five large pictures," said Julian. "The thing is, if you think about it, what could be better for Jared than the arrival of this project? His wife has left him and liberated him of all his domestic ties. Now he can become an artist again. So find we profit by losing of our prayers," he quoted with a faint smile. "This project arriving is fate. It's created a watershed in Jared's life. Fate is willing him to regain himself as an artist. Whether or not he rises to the challenge is in his own hands."

30

In the backroom of the studio a precarious peace had been reached. Jared, Julian and Costanza had found a new model upon their return to Florence. Pia was half English, half Italian, a pretty young girl with spirals of thick wavy brown hair who, the moment she climbed up on the model stand and draped robes over her daily attire of denim and cotton, became a woman of great classical beauty. She did not however, unlike her predecessors, Mercy and Tara, inspire in Jared any personal interest. For one thing, there was no question of the demure slim-hipped girl posing nude. If he wanted to return to his Eve he would not be able to use Pia. She was very much Julian's muse. Never, in fact, had Jared seen Julian quite so flirtatiously high-spirited. Julian was constantly fussing over the young girl, rearranging the folds in the silver Madonna robe over her shoulder or altering the way her hair fell down over the slight incline of her breasts.

If at times Jared felt like a guest in his own studio he did have to admit that the gentle vegetarian girl made a splendid Madonna. He was putting the final touches to the small study of the Immaculate Conception when he changed his mind about the design of the Madonna's hands. Having first painted them pointing down, he then painted them pointing up. For a while she had four arms.

"She looks like the goddess we worship at our community," Julian said. "Lakshmi. Like Venus, she was born of the ocean and inspires in Vishnu everlasting desire."

As the preliminary sketches were nearing completion, Jared learned the project would have to be abandoned.

"I don't understand," said Julian.

"Well, for one thing, we've been undercut by another artist who's willing to do the five paintings for a third of the price. And for another thing, the bishop has qualms over spending so much money on decorating the church. He said, what about the poor? I was tempted to quote the Bible. You know that passage where Magdalene has anointed Christ's forehead and the disciples ask if the money the oil costs might not be put to better use to help feed the poor and Jesus says, the poor will always be with us."

Julian was clearly disappointed and even slightly resentful.

"I was always told there would be no problem raising the money," he said. "The town is full of rich tycoons who by donating the money are exempt from paying some tax or another; it's not even as if they're losing out."

"But then there's this other artist – he's an Asian. What are we going to do about him?"

"What does an Asian know about this tradition? Do they not realise that what we'll produce are five paintings of exceptional quality?"

"I thought you were all for the East?"

"That's not the point. He's not had the training you have."

"Probably not. But we cannot do this project for a third of the price."

"I think we should paint the pictures anyway. Why let all our hard work in designing them just go to waste?"

Jared though was secretly pleased the project had fallen through, feeling it would have been the death of him as an artist. It was always, he thought, more Julian and Costanza's project than his. But then Julian had found a pigeon, he had not found a swan. And what it has meant is that for the second time I've had to abandon my Eve.

Thinking of the two panels of Adam and Eve he intended adding, Jared, now alone in his backroom, studied his picture. He looked at the right arm of Christ. It was pointing down at the oblivious face of his wife, almost as if seeking to pull her out of the world of darkness that had claimed her. The arm was point-ing to the descent - anticipating the harrowing of hell. Christ was extending the right hand to Adam and Eve. He was descending into the crucible, beginning his night sea journey. Jared looked at his wife supine in the low darker realm of the painting beneath the fiery skyline, a yellow rose nestled in her opened palm. She had been plummeted down into an unconscious sleep whereas his Christ, in the throes of descending from his cross, was very much alive.

As he stood back, beneath the statue of Venus, he perceived in his painting the motif of the eternal wheel. The central figures in the picture formed a circle - the rhythm of Christ's body suspended slantwise on the cross was picked up by the fallen Magdalene on his left whose curving body led the eye along the arc of the sleeping Madonna with her raised head; over his wife, and constituting and completing the fourth element of the circle, stood John, supporting the cross in his fiery red robes with the fierce questing intensity in his uplifted eyes. Jared thought of the rose-window of a Romanesque church he had once seen - there had been depicted a wheel around which figures descended and ascended with, on the one side, Fortuna who was cranking the wheel and, on the other, Sapienza. The tiny figure at the apex wore a crown and held a sceptre, and an inscription at intervals around the eight-spoked wheel read:*regno, regnavi, sum sine regno, regnabo.* The king, subject to the wheel, had to descend into destitution in order to ascend back onto his throne.

"How's Excalibur, Edward?" asked Jared, studying his student's painting of Rowan. "Are you still wielding the sword, or have you thrown it back into the lake?"

Edward mock-fenced with his paintbrush and then grew embarrassed and hung his head.

"The sword, you know, is the cross," said Jared. "There's that line. *Think not that I am come to send peace on earth; I came not to send peace but a sword.* Except the sword has been thrown into the lake. It's been dismembered. But we have the metals on our palette. We're using base metals to create spirit. How does that quote go? Yet some say that Arthur is not dead but that he shall come again and win the Holy Cross. *Hic iacet Arthurus, rex quondam rexque futurus.* Here lies Arthur, once and future king. But he never saw the grail, did he?"

"Perceval saw the grail," said Edward.

"Perceval though took it home with him," said Seamus. "He did a runner with it."

"He never took it back to Camelot?" asked Jared. "The quest has to be undertaken all over again? But let's have a look at your painting, Edward. Algernon you drew last term with a huge chin and no forehead. Rowan you've drawn with a huge forehead. He does have a large forehead because Rowan is a bright guy but he also has a stronger chin. You know what they say, don't you? The size of the forehead determines the level of intelligence and the size of the chin determines the strength of will. You've deprived Rowan of his will. Do you have a strong will, Rowan, or are you a passive laisser-faire guy?"

"If I had the choice I don't think I'd ever leave my room except life has decreed so far that I never really have a room of my own."

"Actually, Edward, this is a very fine painting. But can you please give Rowan a little more chin?"

Half-way up the steps to San Miniato Rowan changed his mind and entered the Rose Garden. Blood-red freesias, dusty violets and flowers with pink-veined upper lips and heart-shaped leaves heightened the yellow of the young lemon trees in their earthenware pots. The sloping winding paths led him past a variety of rose bushes, whose names he looked at as he descended the gravel path towards the fountain - Sea-Foam, Nausicaa, Ophelia. The letter he held in his hand, he knew, was from Milena. Before opening it, he tried to imagine what she might have to say for herself. The last thing he wanted to hear was any kind of apology beneath a self-vindicating paean to the treasures of her relationship with Algernon. That was never a relationship he would be able to take seriously and to ask him to do so was an affront to his knowledge of her.

Sitting down on the grass he took off his shoes and barefoot opened the envelope. Behind the uneven broken battlements of the city wall and a tumbling slant of orange rooftops, Florence lay sheathed in a heat haze.

Dear Rowan,

I've been down on my knees all day scraping the crust off an ancient stone wall. Now we've just finished supper. I'm sitting in my room by an open window. The moon seems much bigger here than at home. I'm always exhausted when I slip between the sheets and never lie awake worrying about things. Nor have I once had my nightmare in which I'm chased by a man who wants to cut me with a knife or a pair of scissors.

I'll tell you what we found in our trench. First of all, we found sealed jars of grain which had been buried by passing nomads. Then we dug down to a depth of about a metre and we stumbled upon the skeleton of a small child. I remember Professor Notman was theorising with his assistant as to how it had come to be buried so unceremoniously but I couldn't help trying to imagine the face it had while it was alive. I began to cry. It was the first time I've really cried since leaving Florence. I felt better after having cried, as if something hard and treacherous in me had melted. I ended up brushing the dust from the child's skeleton myself and I gently touched its head and in that moment life seemed to me more wonderful and terrible and utterly mystifying than ever before.

The walls of earth separating the initial trenches began to disappear as new trenches were cut and new stairways and gangways appeared. We began finding all sorts of beautiful things - bracelets of beads, copper pins, the fragments of painted pottery, bowls and jars, shells, needles made of bone, a necklace and one or two rings. We concentrated on a building at the centre which soon revealed itself to have been destroyed by fire. It consisted of several rooms and a large courtyard where there was a well. I felt instinctively that the building had been a special place - a place of music and dance.

Last night I walked alone through the old stone streets, sat on the blackened walls under the stars and went back over my entire life. I suppose this is why I'm writing to you tonight. Things that were important have a habit of springing to mind here. It's as if I've lost all track of time and everything I remember seems only just to have happened.

Today, Professor Notman has found a burial chamber and unearthed the skeletons of a male and a female lying side by side. He believes them to be a royal pair. I thought of Jared and how passionately interested he was in Ulysses and Penelope. I still haven't read that damn book!

One thing I didn't tell you in Florence is that while my mother was there visiting she told me my father wasn't my real father. This news came as a complete shock though thinking about it now I realise there was always a sense of me and him trying too hard with each other. In Florence I blacked out the knowledge which maybe explains why I began acting slightly out of character. I didn't know any more what my character was. All I did know is that I did not want to have to think very much. You always made me think - often in a good way, sometimes in a counterproductive way. It makes me sad that I left without saying goodbye to you. I hope you are well.

Love, Milena.

The grass Rowan's hand had been resting on sprang back up as he finished reading Milena's letter. He looked more closely at the people sitting on the slope below and then noticed a peacock feather lying by the fountain. He remembered the dance of the male peacock at the farmhouse in France, a parody perhaps of male sexual vanity though Julian had later told him that the peacock was a symbol of rebirth as a result of its ability to produce a new plume of bright evanescent feathers every year. He watched as, further down the grassy slope, two girls got to their feet. Like a ballerina, the more beautiful of the two bent down from the waist without arching her legs and picked up a thin scarf which she tied round her hips. She walked over to the fountain and cupping her hands splashed water up into her face. Just then she became aware he was watching her. He took her in at a glance before shyly averting his eyes. It was now he noticed the old man with the limp he had first seen at San Miniato. He was sitting on a wooden bench at a curve in the gravel path, a walking stick propped by his side. Once again Rowan felt a desire to talk to him, to ask him a question.

"*Mi scusi,*" said Rowan. "*Una volta Le ho visto sotto San Miniato e...*"

"Sit down," said the man, studying Rowan closely. "My name is Francis Waterstone."

"Rowan Fisher," said Rowan.

"That ring was once in my possession," he said, caressing the round red stone with the tip of his finger. "I gave it to my daughter."

"Was her name Ivana?"

31

From the shade provided by the statue of Dante, Francis could see the former bedroom window, boarded up behind grey shutters, of his daughter. So Rowan had reappeared - a living incarnation of himself as a young man. What was he going to tell his grandson? How make sense of his history?

When Bianca came to his bedside after Giuliana's death it had been only natural to show her the bullet wound in his thigh. They had slept in each other's arms. The birth of a child might have been, should have been, a bond between two people suffering a shared loss. Instead Francis had foregone in his mind any right to a future that fatal day in 1944. His daughter had always remained the child of his shame at the part he played in Giuliana's death and as such he had neglected her. Had he been a better father might Ivana still be alive?

Ivana Ashworth had not spoken to her husband for three days. This was nothing out of the ordinary. Frequently he vanished for weeks at a time. She had ceased to dwell on his betrayals and rarely confronted him with recriminations. But having for the first time listened to her mother's account of the events which had led to her conception she felt how little credit her life did to the complex act of fate which had enabled her to be born. She was the offspring, she sought to believe, not so much of a loveless couple, but of the love those two people bore for a tragically killed third person. Someone had had to die for her to be born.

This however did not change the fact that her own marriage was a sham.

On the day of the party children had been playing in the piazza when she looked up to see a vaguely familiar blonde girl smiling at her.

"Hello. You're Max's wife, aren't you? Do you remember me? We met at the Corsini's the other evening."

How often now she was referred to, identified as Max's wife. He had even stolen her name, her right to individual consideration.

"Are you going to the party tonight?"

"What party?" asked Ivana.

"It's being held at this Italian sculptor's studio in Borgo San Frediano."

The party was in full swing when Ivana arrived. Flashing coloured lights slid over the floor and tall ceiling of the large oval room. A few people were dancing while the majority lined the walls, sipping wine from paper cups. Max, distracted for a moment from the blonde girl giggling into his ear, shot Ivana a fierce hounded look. She ignored him and struck up conversation with a bearded young American student who spoke agonisingly slowly as if methodically censuring every word before allowing it to represent him.

Before long Max came skulking over and interrupted what had been a laboured conversation.

"What are you doing here?" he demanded.

"Are you worried I'm going to spoil your fun?"

"Fun?" he sneered. "Is that what you think of me?"

"Tonight I don't think I think anything of you, Max."

"Who was that dreadful bore you were talking to? He looked like a gravedigger."

"You're my gravedigger, Max."

"Touché," he mocked.

"So which one of these lovely girls have you got your eye on tonight?"

"I thought maybe young Mrs. Cripwell over there."

"I can see why she would attract you."

"And why would that be?"

"Because she looks pure and you can't stand virgin snow."

"I can't imagine her fucking. That's always a challenge. To do something you can't imagine."

"I could never imagine marrying you."

"There you go then. That proves my point. What really is the point of doing anything you *can* imagine?"

"Hello Max, old chap. How are you?"

Max welcomed the intrusion of a third party and Ivana watched him summon the vast resources of charm, no longer ever solicited for her benefit, that he still had in his armoury. The new arrival was a man with windswept hair, an intense stare and an air of hovering as if he might disappear at any moment. Asking herself what he might do in life, Ivana came up with the idea of sorcery.

"I say, everyone in here looks rather like the souls of the dead in one of Dante's circles of hell."

"If you mean everyone is going around in circles I can certainly attest that this is the case with my wife and I. However, I rather think you have far too much imagination for your own good, Damien."

Ivana was struck by the profusion of attractive females at the party, many of whom wore skimpy short skirts, transparent blouses and, at least on the surface, made light of everything their fathers had taught them. She spoke to the woman Max had singled out as tonight's prey. Katherine was Ivana's age and like her, or so she guessed, unhappily married. Though physically very attractive with beautiful grey eyes and thick long hair, she appeared constrained, withheld, slightly brittle.

"Does your husband not mind you being out here in Florence, away from home?" Ivana asked her.

"My husband has his hands full with business commitments for the time being."

"And you don't have children?"

"No, not yet, though I would like to have children at some point."

They were soon joined by a big-boned young Englishman. PJ Leyfield spoke in a loud carefully polished voice and had a habit of rubbing his palms together as if something interesting was perennially on the verge of happening. Katherine drifted away to get another drink, causing the new arrival to flinch with disappointment. Ivana playfully told him off.

"You could at least try to hide the fact that I was the gooseberry," she smiled.

Rather too earnestly, PJ dismissed the idea that she was a poor substitute as nonsense and began telling her how he had spent the afternoon in the Brancacci Chapel sketching the Masaccio frescoes.

Out of the corner of her eye Ivana could not help monitoring her husband's familiar mating rituals. She could tell that Katherine was too timid to take any definite stance but instead offered herself up as a blank canvas which, apart from the occasional faint tremor or stiffness of response, yielded neutrally to his brush strokes.

Before long Ivana could bear the party no more and decided to leave. She tried to catch her husband's eye but he was still busy dancing around Katherine Cripwell.

This was the last she saw of Max until, days later, he returned home. He threw off his jacket and collapsed onto the sofa.

"Don't look at me as though you want an explanation."

"Don't treat me as though I'm your jailer then. Has it never occurred to you that perhaps our marriage is as much, if not more, of a prison for me as it is for you?"

"If it wasn't me you'd merely find yourself in a different prison. What is life after all if it's not a succession of prisons? Every choice we make is a prison. Freedom is three days in a new city - until someone demands an account of you and then you're once again behind the bars of your personal and ancestral history."

"But you invent your personal history, Max. And your ancestral history."

"Only to other people. You don't, do you, think I believe what I say? I just enjoy getting other people to believe it."

"But you do believe what you say. That's your trick, your stroke of genius. For as long as the game lasts at least. You're like a little boy pretending to be a pirate or a prince. For the duration of the game you become what you're pretending to be. Then you enter into that state of disenchantment which follows in the wake of all theatre."

"I'm a fraud, Ivana. Who knows that better than you?"

"How can you be so cynical in such a beautiful city? Doesn't Florence sometimes induce you to think that there might be something more to life than just getting your leg over?"

She watched him twirl the signet ring in circles on his little finger. It was engraved with a family crest featuring a phoenix and a broken cup. All his ghastly insecurities somehow resided in that ring which he chose to flaunt. She had done her best as a woman to instil in Max some confidence. The fact that she had failed sometimes caused her to doubt her womanhood. In many ways Max ended up making her feel like a little girl. Only when he made love to her did he make her feel like a woman - and then stole from her this sense of coming into her female inheritance by treating her with distaste afterwards.

"I'm actually in rather a scrape." He covered his face with his hands as medieval bells began reiterating their claims and censures in the piazza.

"What kind of scrape?"

"What does it matter what kind of scrape? One scrape is much the same as another."

"I'd like to know. Does it by any chance involve that woman Katherine?"

"If you must know, it involves a statue of Venus."

"A statue of Venus?"

"We replaced a statue of Buddha with a statue of Venus and someone got very upset."

"What are you talking about? What statue of Buddha and what statue of Venus and where and who?"

"At the studio. In the backroom there was a statue of Buddha on a plinth. We took it down and replaced it with a statue of Venus we found downstairs."

"I still don't understand."

"Neither do I but the fact remains that I'm in a scrape."

"And where does Katherine fit in?"

"Who said she did fit in? I found her rather tiresome."

"Because she didn't find you attractive?"

"Who says she didn't find me attractive?"

"She's so shy though that she wouldn't have the heart to say so."

"Well then, it serves her right."

"What serves her right?"

"Anything that happens to her serves her right."

"You're not making much sense."

"The fact is, we've got to leave Florence immediately. I don't like it here anymore."

"I'm not leaving Florence. If you want to leave Florence, fine, but I'm staying."

"Florence doesn't want me anymore. Everything and everyone here is so damned earnest."

"So where are you thinking of going?"

"I don't know. I thought maybe Spain. It's cheap in Spain."

Ivana never saw Max again after that night. News later reached her that Katherine Cripwell had been raped at the party. The implication was that her husband was involved. To begin with she felt indignant on behalf of Max. If Mrs. Cripwell wanted to have sex with him, could she not just admit it instead of fabricating some half-baked exonerating lie? Max was capable of being cruel but he had never once resorted to physical violence, not even when she goaded him on. Later, the manner in which people reacted to her had forced her to assimilate the notion as a fact. She sank into a black depression. She could no longer trust her own mind, let alone look after her son.

On the night of November 3, two months after she had been told Rowan was living in Kent with a Mr. and Mrs. Fisher, Ivana was lying awake in bed. Thundering rain, preceded by crackling spears of lightening, continued to efface the usual view from her bedroom window. Whatever she thought about she believed she could almost summon as a physical entity. She turned to the Bible as protection against the dark roaming sorcery of her fear. The great wonder in *Revelations* had tricked her. Expecting some kind of comforting miracle she encountered bottomless pits, stars falling from heaven, devouring floods and a seven-headed beast with ten horns which rose up from the sea. She saw the beast with its red leathery skin rise up before her so clearly that she fled from the room as if borne off by a pair of wings.

The next thing she knew she was standing outside in the piazza, barefooted with a current of water swirling around her calves. The streetlamps went out. Ivana could barely discern through the heavy gusting rain the faint white shimmer of the statue of Dante at the centre of the square. She began walking towards the river, aware that the water was deeper and its current stronger with every step she took. All the windows of the buildings she passed were blacked out and there was no sign of life anywhere. The motherhood of nature had turned vindictive and violent. Instead of fear she now felt overwhelming sadness. She had abandoned her son.

The water flowing down the incline of via de' Benci from the river struck imploringly at her legs. She heard a dog barking and then a pair of shutters opening somewhere close by. She could not bear the thought of human eyes prying on her and waded back into the piazza. The chilling water was precipitously rising. She looked over towards the door of her palazzo. It was then she was knocked off balance by an angry sustained blast of water.

Francis now stood outside the door to the house in via Porta Rossa where Bianca and Giuliana had lived. He felt faint and an icy film of sweat sensitised his entire body; the pain beneath his left shoulder had spread down his arm and made the blood in his arteries ache with a dull torpor. When, at night, he sensed how close death probably was he realised that he had not succeeded in making sense of anything. There were no compensations, no comforts as far as he could see. After Giuliana's death he had awaited the second act of his life. The second act had been an attempt to understand the first act during the process of which he had consumed what he now realised was the greater part of his life. Why then had he been spared? So that this boy Rowan could be born? He could think of no other explanation. And perhaps, in time, if time there was, this might even come to seem a vindication of sorts. Already the boy had brought back to life his memory of Giuliana.

Split figs oozed out their pips beneath their shoes as he and Giuliana made their way down to the lake. There was a smell of burning in the air and a slow rhythmic circulating motion of the water beneath the reeds when once again she scorned his attempt to kiss her. He was at a loss to follow up the gesture. He didn't believe what she was telling him but she had exhausted his resources, his capacity for action.

It was she who had noticed the German patrol combing the countryside and she who had urged him into the water. He allowed her to take his hand and they waded into the lake up to the waist. She pointed to a secluded spot beneath the arching green boughs of a weeping willow and assured him they would only need to keep their heads under the water for a brief moment. She did not know that was his worst fear. It was then they heard the gruff pitiless German voice. They looked around. Five soldiers were pointing guns at them while an officer beckoned them out of the water. Francis had almost been relieved.

Later they were lined up against the broken wall together with eight Italian men wearing the red scarves of the partisan brigade and two women. A sudden gust of wind blew one or two leaves high into the air. Sunlight caught the barrels of the rifles aimed at him. The young Italian next to him repeatedly succumbed to a dry cough. That one could be irritated by such things at the moment of one's death surprised Francis. He had been standing next to Giuliana who unlike the boy was not trembling. He took her hand and caught her eye - she seemed angry. He then focused his eyes on a red poppy growing alone among the tall dry grass behind the soldiers. The boy coughed again and then they fired. Francis fell, though numb to any pain.

Lying face down on the ground, he became aware of the sound of German voices and the weight and stickiness of something pressing down on one of his legs. He was no longer holding Giuliana's hand and there was no movement around him.

Finally he heard the German voices recede. After listening to a quick medley of birdsong he shoved off the dead body of the boy and reached out towards Giuliana. When he turned her over onto her back he saw she had been shot in the stomach and chest. Warm blood was still seeping out through her black dress. He knelt in the blood and dust staring at her mouth, the mouth he had never kissed, and into her eyes bereft of the play of her nature. Not even in death had they succeeded in uniting. He touched the hand he had held and slid the ring from her finger, the ring that graced the beauty of her hands. When he tried to rise to his feet he realised he had been shot in the thigh though how much of the blood on his clothes was his and how much was Giuliana's he did not know.

Outside the house in via Porta Rossa, Francis felt a wet drop on his forehead which he refrained from wiping away. He thought now of Rowan, his grandson, and as he reached Ponte alle Grazie he saw the church of San Miniato glowing gold on the hill, reflecting within its mosaic of Christ the benediction of the sun's dying rays over the city.

32

Jared and Guido Locatelli descended the stone steps together. The threshold guardian blocking the entrance to the crypt had been moved aside. Lit by the candle Jared held, shimmering reflections of water made the stone arches seem to perform a choreography of mesmerising movement. His own shadow, under the dominion of the candle's flame, loomed consequentially over the arcaded vault. A few inches of water lay over the uneven stone floor and reflected as a blurred glow the flame of the candle.

"Is it possible that this water is left over from the flood?" asked Jared.

"It certainly feels as if time has stayed still down here," said Guido who had remained on a step half-way down.

"I think you should leave it open from now on. It's part of the church's patrimony and as such should be respected. And it is rather wonderful in its way."

Jared ventured into the shallow water to explore the outer reaches of the echoing vault. As he held the candle up to the arched columns he thought of his painting which for five years he had worked on directly above this underground sanctuary. He had begun a sacred image and a series of signs had both heralded and thwarted the undertaking. Then the idea of completing his picture with the panels of Adam and Eve had occurred to him. His own Eve, his wife, had taken him down into the underworld where she was held prisoner by all the darkness in her mind. He had not been able to save her. What perhaps she had done though was to free him as an artist. Yet he had not taken advantage of his freedom. He had spent almost a year sculpting the German tramp Hans as a Bible prophet. And because he had not cast it, the sculpture was beginning to crack, creating the need to repeat work he had already done. The bust had become a kind of Sisyphus stone and Jared's insistence on doing nothing else a criticism levelled at him. In the meantime his Eve picture stood facing the wall, unfinished but never quite forgotten. His artistic life, he realised, was bound up with the Adam and Eve canvases. If he were to make sense of Diane's betrayal he had to act as an artist and until he finished his Eve he would paint nothing but landscapes and head studies. As he returned back up into the light of day he held in his mind a vivid painted image of Adam and Eve - through them, through putting them on canvas, he could redeem not only his art but his life.

Upon the death of his grandfather, Rowan learned that he was to inherit Francis Waterstone's home behind San Miniato. Biana Monaco, his grandmother, had not attended the funeral nor had he seen her again. The first night in the house he felt like an intruder. His grandfather was so overwhelmingly present in its furniture, artefacts and scents that Rowan had to talk to himself to reaffirm his own identity. He avoided looking into mirrors for fear of seeing the old man's face superimposed upon his own. The next morning Rowan unpacked. The letter from Milena was at the bottom of his suitcase. He placed it in the drawer of an old mahogany desk at which he also wrote his first letter.

His new home became a source of invigorating wonder. He rooted through all the old photographs and journals. The more he saw and read the more intimately and fatefully implied he felt in his grandfather's personality. To have discovered this ancestral thread back into the past was to realise that something was expected of him. He understood that everything in the house was now his responsibility and sought to ascribe to every object and memento a continuing fate. His first act was to have four cherrywood frames made for his favourite photos – the one of Milena he nearly tore up, one of his grandfather as a young man wearing a long grey overcoat in front of the church of San Miniato; one of Giuliana, frozen into a kind of fluid question mark while dancing her role in Martha Graham's *Primitive Mysteries;* and one of his mother as a young woman in a long white dress with both hands on her head, entangled in her dark hair.

Walking down Borgo San Jacopo one day, Rowan was surprised to see Michael carrying a paint box and a palette.

"You're back in Florence then?"

"I'm going to teach at the studio again. Things weren't going too great at home. I was working on construction sites. Better to be back at Serristori with the broken pipes and cold water. How's Jared?"

"You haven't seen him yet?"

"I just got in yesterday. I'm on my way to see him now."

"He's fine. He seems a lot calmer."

"His dark night of the soul is over?"

"He speaks less of his wife and more of his art."

"Is he painting?"

"No. He's been sculpting Hans," said Rowan, gesturing towards the portico of the church where the German tramp sat on the steps engrossed in cutting up newspapers with a pair of scissors.

"Does anyone know why he does that?"

"Jared calls him Old Father Time. He thinks his scissors are his scythe and the things he cuts out are obituaries of people who have not yet died."

"So Jared is still turning everyone into archetypes."

"Of course."

"What happened to Julian and Costanza? Are they still in Florence?"

"Apparently Julian has gone back to his guru at the community and Costanza has gone back to her castle though no one is quite sure for how long."

"What about Damien?"

"He's vanished off the face of the earth."

Michael found Jared in the backroom of the studio. The dog was curled up asleep underneath where the portrait of the blind man used to hang. Jared had grown critical of it and taken it down. In front of the Descent from the Cross, Michael told his mentor about his new tattoo. It was just before he booked his flight that he decided to have the cross, which he designed himself, tattooed on his back. The cross, stretching from the base of his spine almost to his neck, fascinated Jared.

"Our cross is also our fate so you're carrying yours on your back. Is that wise?" Jared asked him when Michael stripped off his shirt in front of the big painting, opposite which stood his two panels of Adam and the unfinished Eve.

"I see it more as a talisman," said Michael.

"And as I recall you believe literally in angels and demons?"

Michael nodded. Jared looked at the cross in his picture which presided over his family. His family was now dispersed.

"You know Diane has just had a baby girl? She's called it Vittoria. Victory. There's now no way back, ever."

"I'm sorry," said Michael.

Jared lowered his eyes. "I've got to go and do the rounds, but we'll meet up later. We've got a great group of students here now. More serious. And very talented. The partying has died down."

"That's good," said Michael.

"The studio is still overrun by the British. You're not going to wig out on me again?"

Michael shrugged his shoulders. "I love the British now."

Jared went down to the cast room. Yesterday, while out painting in the Tuscan hills, he had met a priest who was restoring an old abandoned monastery. He told Jared he intended taking care of a number of people with problems. The priest had struck Jared as a kind generous man and left him feeling better about himself. Many people had commented on the healing nature of his atelier - once and even still, thought Jared, the church of the Archangel Raphael, healer and guide of wayfarers.

The two English girls he was critiquing now were called Lucy and Camilla - the name Lucy, he knew, meant light; Camilla meant handmaiden but was also a warrior maiden in the *Aeneid*. While he pointed out the flaws in Camilla's drawing of Donatello's Christ, Jared noticed a beautiful girl with long auburn hair sitting in a model's chair at the far end of the dark room. Her hands were folded in her lap and she was wearing an old-fashioned white cotton dress and the most unusual shade of lipstick. She reminded him of the sculptures of Greek maidens he had seen in Athens as a young man - the korai. Even the colour of her lips - rose madder, he deemed it - suggested the faint traces of paint sometimes surviving on the archaic statues. Kore was always clothed, always suggested an idea of female innocence and spring-like possibility. He was impatient now to reach her and quickly concluded his critique of Lucy's drawing.

"Now then, Ivor," he said, "for a first portrait drawing this isn't at all bad except you've in no way done justice to this girl's beauty. Where did you find your model?"

"She's a friend of Sophie's."

"Does she speak English?"

"I'm American," said the girl from her pedestal.

"What are you doing in Florence?"

"I'm studying bel canto. I want to be an opera singer."

"Won't you have to put on rather a lot of weight?" Jared asked.

"That's just a cliché about female opera singers. Look at Maria Callas. She had a beautiful figure."

"Indeed she did. Is that who you model yourself on?"

"My favourite singer is actually Renata Tibaldi."

"How long are you staying in Florence?"

"Perhaps forever. I adore it here. It's like home away from home."

"I'd love to paint you, if you're free."

"I'd be honoured," she said.
"What did you say your name was?" Jared asked.
"My name's Eve," she smiled.

Acknowledgements

For inspiration, sustenance and feedback, thanks to:

Charles Cecil, Freddie de Rougemont, Georgiana Calthorpe, Talitha Stevenson, Emily Pennock, VJ Keegan, Rupert Alexander, Justin Sparrow, Anna von Kanitz, Paola Rosà, Gina Monaco, Tim Binding, Alex Preston, Judith Kinghorn, Annabel Merullo, Charlie Campbell, Christabel Brudnell-Bruce, Charlotte Raymond, David Flusfeder, Linda Thomas, Kerrie Ashworth, Paolo Cristellotti, Charlotte Cecil, Cristina Zamagni.